His Human Slave

An Alien Warrior Romance

By
Renee Rose

Originally published in Human Surrender,
the dark alien romance box set
Copyright © July 2016 His Human Slave
by Renee Rose

All rights reserved. This copy is intended for the original purchaser of this e-book ONLY. No part of this e-book may be reproduced, scanned, or distributed in any printed or electronic form without prior written permission from the authors. Please do not participate in or encourage piracy of copyrighted materials in violation of the author's rights. Purchase only authorized editions.

Published in the United States of America
Renee Rose Romance

Editors:
Kate Richards, editor—His Human Slave

This e-book is a work of fiction. While reference might be made to actual historical events or existing locations, the names, characters, places and incidents are either the product of the authors' imaginations or are used fictitiously, and any resemblance to actual persons, living or dead, business establishments, events, or locales is entirely coincidental.

This book contains descriptions of many BDSM and sexual practices but this is a work of fiction and as such should not be used in any way as a guide. The authors and publisher will not be responsible for any loss, harm, injury or death resulting from use of the information contained within. In other words, don't try this at home, folks! □

Table of Contents

Chapter One 4

Chapter Two 13

Chapter Three 45

Chapter Four 60

Chapter Five 80

Chapter Six 96

Chapter Seven 99

Chapter Eight 133

Chapter Nine 161

Chapter Ten 164

Epilogue 183

Acknowledgements 189

Chapter One

Zandian Breeding season.

That was the last consideration in his mind before liberating his planet from the Finn.

Breeding season.

Zander sat at the round platform, studying the faces of the elders he respected most, the ones who had risked their lives to save him when the Finn invaded Zandia and wiped out the rest of their species solar cycles before.

"You can't be serious."

"Dead serious," Daneth, the only Zandian physician left in the galaxy said, tapping his wrist band. "You are the best male representative of the Zandian species, the only one left of the royal bloodline, and, more importantly, the only one young enough to produce healthy offspring. If you go to battle without first procreating, our species will die with us." He gestured around the room at the other members of his parents' generation.

He leaned back in his chair and closed his eyes in exasperation. "And exactly which female do you think I will produce these offspring with? Last I heard, there is no Zandian female under the age of sixty left alive."

"You will have to cross-breed. I purchased a program and entered your genetic makeup. It uses all the known gene files in the galaxy to predict the best possible mate for breeding.

He raised his eyebrows. "So have you already run this program?"

Daneth nodded.

He glanced around the table, his gaze resting on Seke, his arms master and war strategist. "Did you know about this?"

Seke nodded once.

"And you approve? This is foolish. My time should be spent training with the new battleships we bought and recruiting an army, not..." He spluttered to a stop.

"The continuation of the species is paramount. What is the point of winning back Zandia if there are no Zandians left to populate it?"

He sighed, blowing out a breath. "All right, I'll bite. Who is she? What species?"

Daneth projected an image from his wrist band. The image of a slight, tawny-haired young female appeared. "Human. Lamira Taniaka. She's an Ocretion slave working in agrifarming."

A human breeder. A slave.

Veck.

Zander didn't have time for this excrement. "There's been a miscalculation." He waved his hand at the hologram.

"No, no mistake. I ran the program several times. This female bested every other candidate by at least a thousand metapoints. This female will produce the most suitable offspring for you."

"Impossible. Not a human. No." Humans were the lowest of the social strata on Ocretia, the planet where his palatial pod had been granted airspace.

"I realize it seems an unlikely match, my lord, but there must be some reason her genes mix best with yours. The program is flawless."

"I thought you might suggest someone worthy of formal mating—an arranged marriage with royalty of another species.

Not a breeder. Not a *pet*." Humans were not mates, they were slaves to the Ocretions. An inferior species. He hadn't had much to do with them, but from what he understood, they were weak, fragile. Their lifespan was short; they did not recover easily from injuries. They spread disease and died quickly. They lacked honor and fortitude. They lied.

Zandians—his species—never lied.

"I was not seeking a lifemate for you—I found the best female for producing your offspring. If you wish to find a mate, after you have bred, I will search the databases for the female most compatible to your personality and lifestyle preferences. But this is the one you must breed. And now, during the traditional Zandian breeding season."

He closed his eyes and shook his head. The breeding season didn't matter. For one thing, they weren't on Zandia—weren't affected by her moons or her atmosphere. For another, he wouldn't be breeding with a Zandian female coming into cycle.

But Daneth was like a sharkhound on a hunt—he wouldn't stop until the stated goal had been reached. He'd been his father's physician and had served on Zander's council as a trusted advisor since the day they'd evacuated Zandia during the Finn's takeover. Zander had been only fourteen sun-cycles then. He'd spent the last fifteen sun-cycles working every day on his plan to retake his planet. He'd settled in Ocretia, where he'd amassed a small fortune through business and trade, making connections and preparing resources, training for war.

"I will take care of everything. I will purchase her and bring her here until you impregnate her. Once it's done, you can send her away. I'm certain you'll be satisfied with the results. The program is never wrong."

"She's human. And a slave. You know I don't believe in keeping slaves."

"So set her free when she's served you." Lium, his tactical engineer spoke.

"A slave will have to be imprisoned. Guarded. Disciplined."

"She's beautiful. Would it be such a hardship to have this woman chained in your bedroom?" This from Erick, his trade and business advisor.

Beautiful? He looked again at the holograph. Dirt covered her hands and cheeks, her unkempt hair pulled back and secured at her nape. But, upon closer inspection, it seemed Erick was right. She was pretty—for a human. Her tangled hair was an unusual copper color and wide-set green eyes blinked at the imager that had captured her likeness. A smattering of light freckles dusted her golden skin. She wore drab, shapeless work garments, but when Daneth hit a command to remove the clothing and predict the shape of her naked body, it appeared to be in perfect proportion—round, firm breasts, wide hips, long, muscular legs. His horns and cock stiffened in unison.

Veck.

He hadn't had that reaction to a female of another species before. He'd only grown hard watching old holograms of naked or scantily clad Zandian females from the archives.

For the love of Zandia.

He didn't want a human. He wanted the impossible—one of his own species, or, if not, then a female of a species that was on the same level as his own, not inferior.

"Why do you suppose her genes are best? What else do you know about her?"

"Well, there's this." Daneth flashed up a holograph of a human man, dressed in combat gear, a light ray gun in his hand, blood dripping from his forehead. "He was her father, a rebel warrior who fought in the last human uprising before her birth. He may even have led it."

"Hmm." He made a noncommittal sound. His species were warriors. Why would he need the human genome for that? "What about her mother?"

"Not much to be found. She's still alive—they're together now, working on Earth-based plant and food growth production. Keeping their heads down, is my guess. The data about her father isn't in the Ocretion database file. My program gene-matched to give me that information. I'm surprised the Ocretions don't do more gene study."

"I'll probably split her in two the first time I use her. Humans aren't built for Zandian cocks."

"The program can't be wrong."

He sighed. "Is she even for sale?"

"No, but you are highly esteemed royalty and the unofficial ambassador from Zandia. I'm sure she can be purchased for the right price." Daneth referred to his position on the United Galaxies. Since the Finns were not recognized by the UG due to their genocidal practices, Zander served as the Zandian ambassador. Not that it did much good. No one on the UG was willing to put their resources behind him to overthrow the Finns.

He made a grumbling sound in his throat. "Fine. But don't spend too much. Our resources are needed for recruiting soldiers."

"Your offspring are top priority. Even over the war plans," Seke said. The male didn't speak often, and when he did, it always had a definitive ring to it, as if his was the last and only word.

"As you wish. I'll breed her. But if she doesn't survive the first coupling, her death is on all of you."

Daneth chuckled. "Humans aren't that weak."

~.~

8

Lamira crouched beside the row of tomato plants and flicked a bug off the leaf before anyone saw it. The Ocretion foremen always wanted to spray the plants with their chemicals at the first sign of any bugs, even though it had been proven to harm the plants.

Her stomach rumbled. She longed to pluck just one juicy tomato and pop it into her mouth, but she'd never get away with it. She'd be publicly flogged or worse—shocked. The fresh Earth-based fruits and vegetables they cultivated were for Ocretions. Human slaves had to live on packaged food not fit for a dog.

Still, her life was far better than it might be in another sector, as her mother always reminded her. They lived in their own tent and had little contact with their owners after working hours.

It might be worse. She could be a sex slave like the sister she'd never met, her body used and abused by men every day. After the Ocretions took her sister, her father had led a human uprising, which had resulted in his death. Her mother, pregnant with Lamira, had been picked up by slave smugglers and sold to the agrifarm. Her mother had been careful to hide her beauty and taught her to do the same, keeping mud on her face and hair and wearing clothes too big. They hunched when they walked, ducked their heads when addressed, and kept their eyes lowered. Only in their own ragged tent did they relax.

"You, there—Lamira." A guard called her name.

She hunched her shoulders and lifted her head.

"The director wants to see you."

Her heart thudded. What had she done? She was careful, always careful. By the age of seven her mother had taught her to distinguish what was real—what others knew—and what was claircognizance. She'd learned to keep her mouth shut for fear she'd slip up and say something she knew about someone without having been told. Had she made a mistake? If she had, it would mean certain death. Humans with special traits—anything abnormal or special—were exterminated. The Ocretions wanted a population they could easily control.

She dropped the bushel of tomatoes and walked up to the main building, showing the barcode on her wrist to the scanner to gain admittance. She'd never been in the administration building before. An unimpressive concrete slab, it felt as cold and dreary inside as it appeared from the outside. One of the guards jerked his head. "Director's office is that way."

The gray concrete floors chilled her dirty bare feet. The director was a fat, pasty Ocretion female with ears that stuck straight out to the sides and cheeks as paunchy as her belly. Beside her sat a male of a species she didn't recognize.

"Lamira." The director said her name, but didn't follow with any instructions.

She stood there, not sure what to do. She tried for a curtsy.

The humanoid male stood up and circled her. He stood a head taller than a human, but unlike the doughy Ocretions, he was all lean muscle. Tiny lines around the outsides of his eyes and mouth told her he might be middle-aged—whatever that meant for his species. Two small horns or antennae protruded from his head. "She's in good health?"

The director shrugged. "I wouldn't know."

The male lifted her hair to peer under her ponytail. He lifted her arms and palpated her armpits. His skin was purplish-peach, a nice hue—an almost human color. His interest in her seemed clinical, not sexual, more like a doctor or scientist.

"What is this about?" she asked.

The male raised an eyebrow, as if surprised she'd spoken.

The director touched the fingertips of her four-fingered hands together. "They are not house-trained, the humans we keep here. They're mainly used for outdoor agricultural work."

House-trained. What in the stars does that mean?

He cupped her breasts and squeezed them.

She jerked back in shock.

"Stand still, human," the director barked, picking up her shock-stick and sauntering over.

Lamira froze and held her breath. She hated the shock-stick more than any other punishment. She'd heard if you got shocked enough, permanent paralysis or even death may result. In her case, she feared she might say something she shouldn't while coming out of the daze from it.

"I'll take her. We'll require a full examination to ensure her good health, of course, but if everything seems in order, I will pay for her."

The director folded her arms across her chest. "Well, we weren't planning to sell her. I understand Prince Zander has a lot of influence with the United Galaxies, but—"

"Two hundred steins."

Her breath caught. Surely they weren't negotiating for *her*—for her life? What about her mother? Her plants? She couldn't leave.

"Three hundred fifty."

Her head swam and she swayed on her feet. No. This couldn't be happening. Her claircognizance should have warned her about this, but it never worked in her favor— only told her meaningless things about other people. A true curse.

"Done." The male punched something into his wristband and a beep sounded on the director's handheld communication device.

The director glanced at it and smiled. "When do you want her?"

The male gripped her upper arm. "I'll take her now." He bowed. "It was nice doing business with you."

She swung around to meet him, terror screaming in her chest. "I can't—wait—"

The male ignored her, pressing a device to the back of her neck.

She felt a sting before everything went black.

Chapter Two

She awoke on her back, naked in a well-lit clinic of some kind. The same male bent over her, taking blood from her arm.

"Ow." She attempted to move her limb but found her wrists and ankles strapped to the table. "Where am I? What are you doing?" Her tongue felt too thick in her mouth.

As before, he ignored her. He injected her blood into a test tube and shook it with a solution then inserted it into a machine and watched the readouts.

When he returned, he put on a pair of protective gloves. He had five fingers, like a human. He wore a lab coat with a name tag that read *DANETH*.

She licked her dry mouth. "Daneth?"

He gazed directly at her for the first time. "It is not your place to address me, slave."

It wasn't her *place*. Right. This must be the "house training" the director had referred to. Though she'd been a slave all her life, other than suffering hard work and poor conditions, she'd escaped the subtleties of groveling indoor slaves were taught. "Are you my master?" She needed to get clear on what was going on.

"No. Your master is Lord Zander, Prince of the Zandians."

Prince of the Zandians. But Zandia had been taken over by the Finn solar cycles ago. So if this man was a ruler, he was king of nothing. Just another wealthy statesman living in exile in Ocrea territory.

"His name is Lord Zander. What, was he named after his planet?"

Daneth brought the pads of his fingers to her right breast, massaging in small circles around the nipple then squeezing it, hard.

She gasped and jerked.

He repeated the action on the other side, checking the readout on his armband, as if following a protocol. With two fingers in her mouth, he pried open her jaws, adjusting the light from his wrist cuff to shine inside.

"Lift your tongue."

It was stupid, but she refused to obey. She'd inherited her father's rebellious mind, she supposed. Knowing he died trying to free his daughters from this exact situation obligated her to resist.

He nudged her tongue up with his finger. She attempted to snap her teeth closed, but he was far too strong, and she only succeeded in straining the muscles of her jaw and throat. Her rebellion did not seem to bother him.

He traveled down the length of her body, palpating every inch. Her nudity felt shocking after a lifetime of baggy clothes. Someone had washed her and even applied a shimmery powder over her skin. Her hair sprawled in soft waves around her head. It, too, had been cleaned and smelled sweet, like citrus blossoms. Violation at being touched so intimately—especially when she'd been unconscious—coursed through her. She had to get out of here. To escape and—

Veck. She didn't even know where "here" was.

She thought they were finished when he unclipped her ankle cuffs, but he only readjusted them, placing her feet in stirrups to lift and spread her legs.

Her bare sex lay open to him for his examination. Her belly quivered, every muscle in her body tense.

"This shouldn't hurt." His tone was matter-of-fact. With his thumbs, he pried open the outer lips of her sex and spread them wide. He prodded her anatomy with a light touch, pulling back the hood of her clitoris as if to make sure it was there.

She whimpered when he shoved two fingers inside her and used his other hand on the outside to massage her inner wall.

"Does it hurt?" He sounded curious, rather than concerned.

"It's not pleasant," she growled through gritted teeth.

He raised his eyebrows, as if the news surprised him. "Hmm." He removed his fingers from her channel and spread her ass cheeks with his thumb and forefinger.

She lifted her bottom in the air, squeezing her back hole against his examination.

He pushed her pelvis back down and pinned it in place with one hand, wiggling a finger into her anus with the other.

She pinched her lips closed on a moan and held her breath, squeezing her eyes closed and willing it to be over. She could get through this. It was a physical examination.

As long as they didn't find out her real secret, she would survive.

~.~

Zander exited the battleship, unbuckling his helmet. Training for war had been a part-time job for him since he was fifteen solar cycles old. The rest of his time was a nightmare of campaigning for support to wage war on the Finn, and keeping up with business to fund the war.

A crowd of servants and advisors stood on the landing deck, waiting to brief him on various aspects of business or the household.

"I have her," Daneth said, dropping in to walk beside him as he strode into the pod.

Veck. The breeder. His new slave.

"Where? Here?"

"In my lab."

"Fine. Bring her to my chamber." *Ugh.* The thought of breeding with another species turned his stomach, but he'd do what he had to do. He entered his chamber and washed up.

When he emerged from the washroom, Daneth had brought the slave. She stood fully nude, except for the wrist, ankle, and neck cuffs he would use to keep her chained up. She crossed her cuffed wrists in front of her sex. Daneth led her by a chain attached to the ring on her collar.

Her jaw was thrust forward, mouth set in an angry slash.

Excrement. No, Daneth couldn't have chosen a meek, submissive human, trained to serve males as a human slave should. This one would be a pain in his ass.

He scanned her body. Fragile. Small. Weak.

How could this human's genes be the perfect mix with his own?

But the sight of her bare nipples, jutted out in stiff points, her flat belly and long, shapely legs did stir his cock and stiffen his horns. Daneth had been right; without the dirt and grime, she was beautiful. Exquisite, even.

But what need did he have for beautiful children? He wasn't bad-looking himself. He needed cunning warriors.

He folded his arms across his chest. "She appears stubborn."

Daneth looked at the data readout on his armband. "Actually, elevated pulse would indicate she's afraid."

She darted a glance at Daneth, as if frightened to hear he was monitoring her vital statistics.

"Then why doesn't she look afraid?"

"Perhaps she wishes to hide it, my lord. Humans often attempt to mask their emotions."

Humans. He had no time for their deceptive ways. "They lie, yes. But it doesn't make sense. If she showed me fear, I would take pity on her. Insolence, I will beat out of her."

The stubborn mask fell away for a moment. *Ah.* There was the fear. So she *had* tried to hide it. Why? It made no sense. And she continued, even after he'd said how he would deal with her attitude.

He reached for her, and she shrank back, attempted to dodge his touch. Daneth yanked her chain forward too harshly, and she stumbled against Zander, her fragile form soft against his body, her skin baby smooth under his hands.

He gripped her upper arms to immobilize her and studied her face. Her eyes were moss-green with yellow starbursts around the pupils. He'd never seen eyes like them before. All of his people's eyes were the same color—brown, rimmed in violet, a complement to their purple-hued skin.

"Are you afraid, slave?"

Her little tongue darted out to moisten her lips, which had cracked. "Yes, my lord."

Finally, the truth. "Good. Learn to please me and we will get along well enough."

"Why am I here?" she croaked.

He glanced at Daneth. "You told her nothing?"

Daneth shrugged. "I thought it best to minimize my interaction with her, as she will be yours to mold and shape."

Stars, he didn't have any interest in molding or shaping any being, much less a human slave. But he supposed Daneth's caution made sense. He would be her master; he would have to be the one to train her to his liking.

He heaved an exasperated sigh. "You're here for breeding."

Her eyes flew wide and she stopped breathing for a moment. Real alarm flitted across her face. Her throat worked to swallow. "I'm not a breeder."

Her lack of deference when she spoke annoyed him. He was used to being treated with the utmost respect by all those around him. "The choice is not yours," he snapped.

Daneth picked up his irritation. "She may require some correction, my lord, but I'm certain she will learn quickly. She was not house-trained by the Ocretions, so her manners require refinement." Of course he wanted this to work, since it was his idea.

Zander released her and crossed his arms once more. "What makes you so certain?"

"Her brain activity is very high for a human. She's intelligent. We already know she has excellent genes."

"I'm not a breeder," she repeated. "I wasn't trained for sex. I'm a virgin."

A virgin. *Veck.* That was the last thing he needed. He already had concerns about his cock fitting into a being so small.

He waved an impatient hand. "Cease the prattle. Do not speak unless you are invited to do so."

She shifted in agitation. "There's been some kind of mistake."

He definitely didn't have time for this. He jerked his horns toward the cage Daneth had installed in his room for her. "Put her in the cage. I'll breed her later."

At the mention of cage, she spun and tried to make a dash for the door. He didn't know where she thought she'd go, considering he had guards at every door in the pod, and the only exit was in an airship.

He caught her around the waist and yanked her back against his body. "Enough," he growled in her ear. Looking to Daneth, he asked, "How do they recommend punishing her?"

"A beating with the flat of your hand on her buttocks should suffice for minor infractions, my lord."

He sat on his sleepdisk and flipped her face down across his thighs, bringing his hand down on her bare bottom.

She inhaled sharply and tightened her cheeks.

He didn't use his full strength, even though it was just his open hand. She was female, and human—he didn't want to cause her real harm, only to quell the rebellion in her. He slapped her upturned backside over and over again, watching as her pale skin turned an enchanting shade of pink.

She squirmed and kicked her legs until he caught her ankles and fastened the cuff clips together. That impeded the kicking.

He resumed the steady beating, wondering how much it would take until she broke. She held her breath then let it out in little gasps and cries. Each time they came out, they sounded more plaintive, but she hadn't yet begun to weep. Humans were emotional creatures, or so he'd heard. Far more emotional than his species. They cried when wounded.

He stopped paddling her and wrapped a fist in her hair to lift her head. Her face was red, but her eyes were dry.

"She's not crying," he said to Daneth. It came out like an accusation. Well, this whole scheme was Daneth's doing, so he should prevent it from being so difficult. "Don't they cry when they're in pain?"

"Yes, well, her vitals indicate stress."

"It is not sufficient. She should be crying."

"There are harsher methods of punishment, but they may cause permanent damage or excessive stress. We want her healthy for breeding."

"Research it further. This isn't working."

"Note the color of her buttocks."

His cock stirred at the mention of her rather attractive posterior. As if he hadn't noticed it already. Her skin had turned a mottled red where he'd disciplined her, and the flesh had already swollen.

"It worked, my lord. She is just stubborn."

He pulled her roughly to stand, out of patience with her deceit, which made no logical sense. Why wouldn't she simply cry and concede to him if the punishment had worked? "Put her in the cage."

Daneth stepped back, as if too squeamish to lift her. He supposed there was some reluctance on his advisor's part to get intimate with the human, if she belonged to Zander.

"Never mind," he muttered. "I'll do it." He scooped her up. She was lighter than he expected. And softer. She smelled sweet, like some kind of flower, but not in an overpowering way. His horns stiffened and turned. His blood warmed. All right, apparently he *could* be attracted to a human.

The truth was, he had little experience with females of any species. He'd been evacuated from his planet when he was a youth, and most of his species had been destroyed in the takeover. He'd experimented a bit with other species as he came into manhood, but Seke had advised him he scattered his energy in doing so—he should keep it for his training. He'd put off breeding until now.

But his slave needed reminding of her place. He'd have time enough to breed her later, if his irritation with her faded. He hefted her through the door of the cage, slamming the door shut behind her.

Unable to move much with both her wrists and ankles bound, she curled up on her side, with her back to him. He saw trembling in her buttocks and thighs. Yes, Daneth was right. The punishment must have had its effect. Too bad she hadn't learned from it.

"I'll leave you, my lord, unless you require anything else?"

"More information on discipline. That is all."

Daneth bowed and left the room.

He flicked on his hologram and checked the daily reports on his trades.

A sniff sounded from the cage.

~.~

Her bottom was on fire. The Zandian prince's hand had fallen like a paddle—stinging her flesh as well as leaving a deeper hurt below the surface—the kind that would leave lasting soreness. She'd kept her emotions at bay during the punishment, but now that it was over, tears leaked down her nose, dripped onto the finely woven carpet in her cage.

Yes, her *cage* had the nicest rug she'd ever seen. Well, apart from the one on Zander's floor. The cage itself was polished hardwood—light in color. Not a wood from Earth—she was familiar with all of those from her work in agriculture. No, this was a very hard wood, sanded and polished until it gleamed. Zander's entire space pod spoke of wealth and opulence. She'd never seen such finery—not even in the holograms she'd glimpsed over the guards' shoulders back on the agrifarm. The rooms and corridors were shaped by domed walls, which were textured and colored in rich, happy shades of yellow, red, and purple. Prince Zander's egg-shaped bed, draped in rich-hued silks, hovered a foot off the floor without any visible means of support. So did her cage. A skylight in the ceiling had a fist-sized crystal embedded in it, which seemed to provide all the natural light the chamber needed. Zander may have lost his planet—or, rather, his father had, if she knew her history—but he still lived like a king.

"Lamira."

It was the first time anyone had called her by her name since she'd been taken from the agrifarm.

The prince's voice was deep and resonant. Commanding. As masculine as a voice got. It reached inside her and made something flutter in her belly.

She ignored the sensation and him.

He spun the cage so she faced him.

She attempted to roll to her back to change sides, but not before he'd seen her face.

"*Now* you're crying."

His powers of observation were overwhelming.

"Why?"

She completed her roll to the other side, away from him.

He spun the cage back so she faced him once more. "Open cage," he commanded, and the voice-activated lock clicked. To her, he said, "Come out."

She didn't move.

His tone went sharp. "Do not anger me a second time, Lamira."

Well, apparently he'd already cowed her completely because his words went straight to her chest, creating a sudden tightening and sending her instantly into motion. She hated how easily he'd mastered her. One stupid spanking and she rushed to please him.

She sniffed back the tears and attempted to push up to her hands and knees—no easy feat with her wrists and ankles bound.

"Release wrist cuffs. Release ankle cuffs," he commanded. They sprang apart but not off.

She backed out of the cage, toward the door, not sure how she would get out until his large hands grasped her waist and lifted her easily to the floor.

Where to look... Certainly not at the prince—her master—although his presence was more than commanding. He stood almost seven feet tall with thick, corded muscles across his chest and arms.

Moisture gathered between her legs.

He looked more warrior than prince. No, he was all king. A warrior king. Earlier, she'd stared at him boldly. Now she kept her eyes lowered, trained at his bare feet. They were no different from hers, except larger and with the brown-purple skin tone of the Zandians. She glanced at her own toes. They were cleaner than they'd ever been before. Even her toenails had been buffed to a glossy shine. How long had she been out?

The prince cupped her chin and lifted her face. His touch was gentler than she expected. She still couldn't meet his gaze, choosing instead to stare at his thick neck and the part of his bare chest visible beneath his loose, finely woven white shirt. Her fingers itched to touch his skin, to find out if it was as smooth as it appeared. What a strange idea. She'd never thought about touching a male in her life. In fact, she'd avoided males as best she could. This one had her completely discombobulated.

Was his chest hairless? Did he have hair anywhere other than his head? Zander, Daneth, and the guards she'd seen outside all wore their hair shorn close to their skulls. Perhaps their horns got too hot otherwise.

When she'd first seen Daneth, she'd thought the horns ugly, but Zander's suited him, somehow making him even more handsome.

He leaned forward and opened his mouth. She tried to pull out of his grasp, but he held her fast, his gleaming teeth aimed straight for her cheek. For a moment, she thought he planned to bite her face, but his tongue flicked out, and he licked one of her tears. She caught his scent, a clean, masculine aroma with a slightly exotic spice.

Her nipples tightened; her pussy pulsed. No—she definitely was not thinking about licking him back to see how he tasted.

He made a sound, almost as if he found the taste of her tears pleasant. "Why are you crying?"

She tried once more to pull away. Not succeeding, she averted her gaze. "I'm not."

Zander switched his hand from her chin to her nape and yanked her up to her tiptoes, until her nose came within inches of his bent head. "Why do you lie?" he snapped. "I can see your tears with my own eyes."

Her eyes filled and spilled again, her lips trembled. She hated crying like this. She shouldn't act so weak. Her father was a revered revolutionary. She and her mother passed messages for the insurgents along a secret human network. But, now—naked, bottom still pulsing with heat, face inches from his, she'd lost all dignity.

She lifted her bound wrists and rubbed them across her eyes. "It's what I wish were true."

He cocked his head. "You wish you were not crying?"

"Right."

"Can you not stop?"

She blew air through her lips. "I thought you were supposed to be the superior species here. Is it so hard to understand?" She immediately wished she hadn't spoken, because his face hardened and his fingers tightened on her neck.

"You will speak with respect." His tone sliced through the air, ice-cold.

She flinched. For once, she swallowed back her pride and said the right thing. "Forgive me."

He blinked as if he was considering whether to believe her. His grip on her nape eased, and he lowered her to her feet. Snapping his fingers, he pointed at the floor. "Kneel at my feet. I work here in my chamber. When I am here, that is the position you will assume."

Everything about her rebelled at the dictate, but she managed to keep her mouth shut and hide her reaction. She dropped to the floor to assume the required pose. The cuffs on her ankles dug into the already raw flesh of her bottom. Her stomach rumbled. She hadn't eaten since the morning she left the agrifarm. She didn't know how long ago that was—how long she'd been unconscious—but her stomach said it had been a long time.

Prince Zander settled in a hover chair beside her and opened a hologram. She watched as he scrolled through numbers and opened messages. A light flashed in the upper right quadrant of the projection. "Connect Daneth."

Daneth's hologram projected into the room "My lord, my monitors indicate the human may require food already. Would you like me to take her to the kitchen? Or have something sent to your room?"

Zander's gaze flicked down at her with impatience. "Is that why your stomach grumbles?"

She nodded. "Yes, my lord." It cost her to speak to him with respect, but she even managed not to sound mocking. If those were the rules of this new life, she would follow them. It was the way her mother had kept them safe and together so long. Head down, feign compliance. Plan a revolution. Besides, she had bigger battles to pick—like avoiding the intended taking of her virginity.

He snatched up the leash and clipped it to her collar, jaw tight, disgust painted across his handsome face. "I'll take her to the kitchen. How often does she require food?"

Daneth winced. "Two to three times a day. And they recommend she have liquids at all times. The lack of fluids may explain why her lips have cracked. I thought it might be our atmosphere, but that's all compatible."

He lifted her to her feet, using the leash, which caused her to choke.

"Ouch," she protested, glaring.

He frowned and shook his head. "Fragile human," he muttered, but her sixth sense registered guilt behind his frustration. He hadn't meant to hurt her.

"How often do you eat?" she asked. There was accusation in her voice, or maybe it was defensiveness. Whatever it was, it offended the prince.

He popped the leash toward him.

She flew forward onto her knees, pain flashing up her neck and into the base of her skull. Lights danced before her eyes.

~.~

Veck and excrement. He bent and picked up the weak human female from where she'd fallen to her knees. Dropping her back on her feet, he rubbed her nape to ease her pain.

He hadn't meant to yank her so hard, had forgotten how little she weighed. Anger at himself quickly morphed into general irritation with the whole *vecking* situation. What was he doing with a *vecking* slave? He hadn't the slightest idea how to train her or care for her well-being. He hadn't even wanted offspring. He didn't want any of this mess.

He unclipped the leash and threw it on the floor. "I don't need this damn leash. You will follow a step behind me or you'll be beaten. Is that clear?" He shouldn't yell at her. It wasn't her fault he'd hurt her.

Her eyes swam with tears, and guilt stabbed at his consciousness.

"Why are you crying?"

"I'm not."

For the love of his species, were they really playing this game again?

He ran his fingers around her collar, checking for wounds. "I hurt you?" Rug burns reddened her knees, but nothing terrible.

She shook her head. "I'm hungry, that's all." Her voice choked with tears.

The sound of it grated on him—made his chest tighten. She affected him in far too many ways. He wasn't an emotional creature by nature. Not like a human. But, in the course of an hour, she'd inspired anger, frustration, and guilt. And yes, lust. Because the sight of her naked body had him itching to *veck* her senseless.

"And you don't wish to cry, but still you do." He growled with impatience and snapped her wrist cuffs together in front of her. "Follow." He marched out of the room. He didn't look back but her light footsteps padded right behind him.

His guards stole surreptitious glances as they passed. For some reason, it made his fists clench. They were lucky none of them openly gawked or he'd have their heads. He glanced over his shoulder and caught Gunt, the guard who stood at his chamber door, staring at Lamira's naked buttocks, which, of course, still glowed, painted red with his handprints. Gunt caught his glower and immediately shifted his gaze to the wall.

He grasped Lamira's elbow and pulled her up to his side.

"You said to walk behind you, my lord," she protested.

"Do not ever argue with me, slave. Your duty is to follow my lead at all times. I may change my mind or directions at a moment's notice. You will adjust."

When she didn't answer, he halted and spun her around to face him, raising his eyebrows.

"Yes, my lord." She sounded sullen, but her eyes remained lowered. It was a small step forward. He waited a moment longer for her to lift her eyes so he could give her a fierce glower of warning.

She blanched.

Good. She would learn. Hopefully sooner than later. He walked her to the kitchen.

Daneth, being the ever-capable advisor, had called ahead, and his servants there had already prepared several possibilities to feed her.

"Will this do, my lord?" Barr, the chef, asked, placing several plates piled with food on the counter. "Master Daneth was not certain what she would eat, but he suggested a few possibilities." The chef's eyes flicked to Lamira's peach-tipped breasts and Zander's horns twitched.

He wanted to throw the plates of food at the male. "She'll eat what we feed her," he growled, but he pushed her in front of the plates and allowed her to choose for herself.

He didn't know what to expect, but she picked the same one he would have picked, had it been his day to eat—a meal of delicate birdflesh with fruit compote over a serving of grain.

She gazed up at him with a question in her eyes. Or was it a supplication? His horns leaned in her direction and his cock stiffened. He enjoyed that look on her. He imagined her on her knees, pleading for his mercy, or for him to grant her a boon. He wasn't sure what it was she wanted now, though.

She dropped her eyes back to her plate and grasped the curved utensil.

He suddenly understood. She wanted her wrists freed to eat.

"Release cuffs."

Oh Zandian sun, she was beautiful. Her smile of gratitude sent a wave of something unfamiliar through the center of his chest. He didn't like it. She was trouble. A pain in his backside. She lied. She deceived. She couldn't control her wild human emotions. She would distract him from his work to no end. The last thing he needed was to feel pity or...anything else for this female.

He did not often visit the kitchen, but there were far more servants crowding into the space than belonged. All of them stole curious glances at Lamira and her naked body.

She ate quickly, as if afraid someone might take the food away from her. She *had* been hungry.

No, he wouldn't feel guilty about that, either.

She finished one quarter of the food on the plate and set the utensil down, pushing the plate away. She flashed a brilliant smile at Barr, the only being who remained in the kitchen now. "Thank you. This is the most delicious meal I've ever had."

He wanted to throat-punch the chef. Which wasn't fair. His entire staff—every being in the pod—was made up of Zandians. Many of them were highly skilled professionals, but they'd chosen to take serving positions to be near him, or perhaps to be near the Zandian crystals in his possession. His species needed them to survive, so, when they'd evacuated Zandia, they'd taken a load of crystal as well.

"Please, my lady...er—" Barr's eyes darted to Zander.

No, definitely not *my lady*. She was far from his mate. But he suddenly didn't want his staff thinking of her as beneath them, either.

"Lamira," he corrected.

Barr bowed. "Lamira, please eat as much as you like..." he trailed off again, once more realizing he'd overstepped his bounds.

Zander gave him a cold stare. "She will require sustenance two to three times a day. She obviously eats very little at a time, however."

Barr bobbed his head. "We will provide her with whatever she wishes."

What emotions twisted around in his chest now? Some odd mixture of jealousy combined with satisfaction. He wanted Barr to care appropriately for his slave, but he didn't like the way she smiled at him.

Stars. Having this *vecking* female created a starstorm of issues in his pod. She was not an honored guest here. She was a slave. Except only for him. "Treat her like a fellow staff member. No higher, no lower. She serves me like you do," he snapped. He swept his gaze around the room, making sure they'd all heard it.

Everyone nodded their assent.

And stared at her breasts.

Excrement. She would not be allowed out of his chamber unclothed again.

~.~

She almost had to jog to keep up with Zander's long strides back to his chamber. He refused to look at her, a muscle flexing in his temple. She couldn't figure out why he'd be angry. She didn't mind hurrying, though. Parading through the halls naked with her freshly spanked ass hanging out for all to see was not her idea of fun. It was utterly humiliating. It also had her sex wet again. Now that most of the pain had faded, the memory of the spanking strangely excited her. She imagined him doing it again, then forcing her to breed.

But no. She didn't want that. She wasn't supposed to want the attention of any male. Which might prove difficult here. From what she'd gathered, there were only males in Zander's pod. And, yeah, the Zandian males were...very masculine. Something about being around so many huge, ripped bodies, giant cocks stuffed in tight pants, and horns pointed right at her while the beings stared at her body had her nipples hard and her pussy damp. It had her skin flushing and tingling. It had her wondering how big and long the Zandian prince's cock might be.

The guard who stood outside Zander's door grabbed her ass when she passed him on her way into the room. No, he didn't grab it. It was more of a grope. A fleeting touch—his fingers brushing her inflamed flesh, questing along her curves.

She turned and glared at him but, he stood staring straight ahead, as if nothing had happened. Should she tell Zander? But, no, he didn't want her speaking unless spoken to.

"Door shut." The door slid closed at Zander's command. "In this chamber, you will always be naked. When you leave this room, you will cover yourself."

She lifted her arms and made a show of searching around her body. "With what?" It was the wrong thing to do—she certainly ought to know better.

But her claircognizance told her Zander wasn't cruel. He wasn't dangerous—not like the Ocretion foremen with their shocking devices. Maybe she sensed that underneath the arrogance and superiority, he was an honorable being. Maybe part of her thought it was fun to goad the prince who thought so little of her species. Or maybe she was just a stupid, crazy female who couldn't suppress her macabre curiosity in receiving punishment at the prince's hand. Because the pain and humiliation of the first spanking he'd given her had left her changed.

His expression hardened. He sat down on the hovering disk that served as his chair, snapped his fingers, and pointed at his feet.

She didn't miss his meaning and didn't have the nerve to pretend she didn't understand. She lowered herself to her knees near his feet.

"Look at me."

She craned her neck to meet his gaze.

"Lamira, you have tried my patience too many times already today. If I am to believe Daneth, you are not unintelligent. If you speak to me in a disrespectful tone again, I will make your earlier punishment seem like a caress. Do you understand?"

She swallowed. "I'm sorry, my lord."

He stared at her for a beat. She gazed into his chocolate brown eyes and realized the outer ring and the pattern within the iris was pure violet. Incredible.

"Humans lie."

"I'm not lying." Was she pushing him too far again? Why couldn't she stop herself?

He slapped her face.

It stung and brought tears to her eyes, even though she knew he might have struck her far harder.

"Why do you continue to fight me?"

"I don't know," she whispered, staring at the finely woven rug as hot tears slid down her burning face.

She wondered about her mother—if she even knew what had happened to her only daughter. If she'd ever see her again. How all this would turn out? Did she truly belong to Zander now? His sex slave? His breeder?

Her father had revolted and given his life over his first daughter becoming a sex slave. It would kill him to know his younger daughter also ended up with that fate, to be a breeder.

She hated the quivering place inside her that found the idea half-arousing. She should not be thinking of how it would feel to be strapped down and taken against her will by a giant Zandian male.

Zander cupped her chin. His touch was surprisingly gentle but still strong and sure. He brushed her tears with his thumb then rubbed it together with his forefingers, as if mystified by the substance. "I don't like when you cry."

She didn't know what he meant by that. Was it an order to stop crying? She swiped at her tears with the back of her hand. Thankfully, he hadn't reattached her cuffs after she'd eaten. She gulped in her breath and held it, trying to stop the tears from flowing. "I'm sorry, my lord."

His fingers wove into her hair. "We eat once a week in Zandian time, which on Ocretia is about ten planet rotations."

She stilled, surprised to hear him answer the question he had scolded her for asking.

"The rest of the time, we get our energy from light. The solar rays are different here on Ocretia than they were on

Zandia, so we use a crystal amplifier for light baths once a week or more."

She didn't often have visions. Usually the curse came as claircognition, not clairvoyance. But, in that moment, she had a flash of the most beautiful rainbow light bathing her skin, making ecstatic ripples of joy shimmer all around her. Gooseflesh stood on her skin.

She swallowed. "Thank you," she whispered hoarsely.

"You're still thirsty," he said. "There's a fluid tube in your cage. You may go and drink from it."

A fluid tube. In her cage.

She wasn't sure she would ever warm up to being kept in a cage like an animal, but there was something oddly comforting about having her own space within this terrifying new reality. When she started to stand, he lifted her with a hand under one arm.

His superior strength made her knees weak. He could hurt her. Far worse than he had. He certainly had shown restraint. Why did that turn her on?

She crawled into her cage and located the tube. The liquid inside tasted sweet and fruity. Delicious. She drank her fill and then crawled back out, settling once more at her master's feet. He didn't acknowledge her, but the tension between them had eased.

She watched him work, listened to his conversations, watched his messages. His large hands moved with elegant grace as he traced holograms, stretching them, shrinking them, sliding to the next one. The same large hands that had paddled her raw.

She longed for him to touch her. There. There it was. The unacceptable truth. He had slapped her face and spanked her ass. He had cupped her chin and gripped her nape. He'd held her arms. But she was his sex slave. His breeder. Shouldn't he be interested in touching her breasts? Her pussy? When would he do so?

A tap sounded at the door.

"Enter."

Daneth came in, followed by two servants carrying various objects. The first one brought a piece of furniture—some kind of bench. The second one carried...oh *veck*. They were instruments of torture. Things to beat her with. Frightening, cone-shaped objects. Various tubes of gels and ointments.

Daneth began explaining them all to Zander, who watched her face as she absorbed it. She tried to keep it blank, but probably didn't succeed. Her ears burned. Her bottom, which had stopped throbbing, tingled. A loud rushing sound in her ears made their voices sound far away.

"Slave, come here," Daneth said.

Zander spoke. "Lamira." It sounded like a correction—to Daneth—and it made something in her chest flutter. Not *slave*. Lamira.

She rewarded the consideration with obedience, stepping forward, even though she knew what would happen. The doctor, or scientist, or whatever he was, pushed her down over the bench, snapping her wrists and ankles to the legs. She lay naked, with her ass lifted and spread, offered up for punishment.

"It can also be used for the breeding, you see," Daneth explained, tapping her sex with two fingers.

She wriggled away.

"Oh, this should also be useful during penetration. It may prevent tearing from your larger size." Daneth roughly smeared something cold and liquid across her folds.

She tightened both holes, straining against her bonds.

"Leave us." Zander's voice sounded even deeper than usual.

34

"Yes, my lord." She imagined Daneth bowing and backing toward the door.

Her legs trembled on the bench. This was it. He was going to shove his enormous Zandian cock in her virgin hole now. Her hands turned cold and clammy. She gripped the legs of the padded bench so hard her knuckles turned white.

It occurred to her to beg—to plead with the prince, who might not be such a terrible being, to postpone their copulation. But her lips wouldn't work, tongue didn't move. She remained silent in the horrible position, offered up to him like the slave she was.

Zander probed her entrance with his finger, rubbing the slick substance around her entrance. He pushed his finger inside.

Her foot jerked, and she sucked in her breath across bared teeth.

"Does that hurt?"

She didn't answer him. No. It didn't hurt, but she didn't want to tell him that. She wanted him to stop, to put her back in the odious cage and leave her alone.

He slapped the back of her thigh, and she yelped. "I asked you a question."

"I don't like it," she said sullenly.

A long silence stretched while he screwed his huge finger inside her. It met her virginal resistance and he paused, going slowly, investigating her interior walls. Her belly fluttered. Heat flooded her sex, flushed out across her skin. Her pussy swelled under his touch, the lubricant spreading with a more pleasing sensation now.

"Your genes, of all those recorded in the Ocreatic galaxy, are predicted to mesh best with mine. I don't know why—it doesn't make sense to me how a human could bear the best offspring for me, but that's what the program says. So neither of us has to like it…but we *are* going to do it." There was a steely dominance to the dictate.

It made something pulse deep inside her. She experienced an opening, a yawning of her sexual organs, as if they accepted his words at face value and wanted to oblige.

She didn't want to oblige, however. This shouldn't be happening to her. She wasn't meant for breeding.

"I know you're small and I'm large. I will do my best not to hurt you."

"No." It sounded stronger than she felt. In her mind, it was a whimper. She knew the inevitability of her fate, here.

He slapped one cheek, hard. "You don't tell me no." He shifted behind her, the rustle of clothing signaling his disrobing. He rubbed the head of his cock against her entrance.

She twisted to catch a glimpse of it, but, from her position, saw nothing but the chiseled muscles of his bare torso, his strength and power almost shocking. No, it was his sex that shocked her. He pushed it in, wedging the huge organ into her tight channel.

"Oh, oh! No, no no," she moaned, her teeth clenched.

"Hush, human."

"Lamira. My name is Lamira, you overgrown alien ape. You think you can—*uhn*—" she broke off as he bumped her ass with his loins, driving deeper, right up against her resistance. "You think you're so superior, you can afford to buy any slave you want—oh, oh *veck*!" He broke her hymen. A brief pain flashed when it tore and then he was deep, filling her with his enormous cock. "No, no, no more."

He reached around and covered her mouth with his hand, moving in and out of her. His breath rasped behind her, rough and labored.

She bit his finger as hard as she could—hard enough to draw blood.

"*Veck!*" He yanked out of her.

She thought she'd feel relief, but her body experienced his loss as a disappointment, even though it had been far too much.

He cursed again and then she had a split second of warning from the whistle through the air before something hard and thin struck her across the ass—across both cheeks.

She screamed and looked over her shoulder. He held a wooden stick of some kind, about a half-meter long and five centimeters wide. The whapping sound it made when striking her flesh sounded nearly as loud as her screams. He beat her with it—ten times in rapid succession.

She wailed as if he were killing her. *Veck*, he might kill her. There was anger and force behind his strokes. Not that she blamed him. She'd certainly inflicted her own damage.

Fortunately, the wooden implement wasn't that thick. It didn't pack a wallop like a heavy wooden paddle. She'd been beaten with one of those once at the agrifarm and didn't want to repeat the experience.

He went still behind her.

She continued to wail, with no semblance of pride now.

"Stop the noise."

She tensed, waiting to see what happened next. Her ass throbbed, the welts he'd laid stinging like a million pinpricks. Her bottom twitched of its own accord. Her sex pulsed, hot and swollen. Moisture seeped from her slit. It must be his fluids—had he finished?

Vaguely, she was disappointed.

No, flesh slapped audibly behind her, but he wasn't touching her. Was he...servicing himself?

~.~

It couldn't have gone worse. He was going to ream Daneth for this idiotic plan. He pumped his cock in his fist, but he'd lost all interest in copulation after the human's ridiculous wails. Daneth must have made a mistake—Zandians and humans were not sexually compatible. He may have been initially aroused at the sight of her bound and presented for his taking, but not anymore.

He closed his eyes and willed himself to a finish. He would reach the point of climax then enter her one more time to deposit his seed. He didn't want to endure any more of her cries than necessary to get this finished.

There. Almost there. He gripped her hips and pushed back inside. She grew even wetter than before, more welcoming. Her muscles gripped his cock.

Stars...*yes*. He shot his load, finishing deep inside her. As soon as it was over, he pulled out and released her from the bonds. The wailing had quieted down to a mewling, panting cacophony.

"Get in your cage." He was utterly disgusted with her. With himself, too. He should have researched this himself, instead of relying on Daneth's knowledge. Perhaps there was something he could have done to prepare the delicate human for a Zandian intrusion.

He turned his back on her, listening as she pushed herself to her feet and crawled into the elevated cage.

"Lock cage," he murmured. "Lights off." With a sigh, he climbed onto his sleep disk and lay on his back with his fingers interlaced behind his head.

Her breathing still sounded ragged, long terraced inhales she held and then let out with a burst. The scent of her tears hit him. Were they fresh? Or from the spanking he'd given her?

He didn't think he'd paddled her too hard. The slender wooden implement had packed more of a wallop than his hand, but it was too light to have left anything more than surface bruising.

She sniffed. Yes, she was crying.

He hated the way her tears made him feel—agitated. Cranky.

Veck, he hated all the feelings the foolish little human invoked. He preferred not to feel, in general. Zandians weren't emotional like humans. He couldn't have her disrupting his life so much.

Another sniff.

Veckety veck veck.

He climbed out of bed and padded over the hand-woven Ostrion rug to her cage. "Unlock cage." She flinched when he touched her ankle, but he laid his hands on her anyway, pulling her out of the enclosure and carrying her to his sleep disk.

"Lights on." He stared down at her.

She blinked, her large green eyes wide and wary. He grasped her wrists and attached the ring on the cuffs over her head to a fastener Daneth had installed.

"No," she wailed, fresh tears starting up again.

"Hush. I'm checking you for injuries. What hurts?" He parted her legs and peered at her sex.

Most of his seed had spilled out of her, coating her inner thighs with the rainbow-hued semen.

That wasn't right. Another sign they were incompatible.

"Call Daneth." He spoke to his processor on the wall.

A hologram of Daneth's face illuminated, hovering before him. Daneth blinked in his dark room. "My lord?"

"I think I inflicted internal damage. She won't stop crying."

Daneth flew out of his sleeping platform. "I'll be right there." A few moments later, he knocked and entered.

Lamira shrank from his physician.

"Why is she afraid of you?" he snapped, his agitation not diminishing.

Daneth arched his brows. It wasn't like Zander to be out of sorts. "I imagine she's tired of being poked and prodded."

The scientist clipped her ankles wide and examined her.

Zander gritted his teeth when Daneth probed her sex, although he wasn't sure if it was because he didn't like it, or her obvious displeasure. "All your seed spilled out of her."

"I saw that," he snapped.

Daneth tapped his lips with a forefinger. "I will research it."

"You'd better. If things don't improve drastically—" he broke off, not wanting to speak about Lamira's future in front of her. She might try to thwart his attempts to breed her if she knew how close he was to writing off the whole project.

Daneth completed the exam and flashed images of her vital statistics and internal organs up for him to see the holograms himself. "There's nothing seriously wrong with her. She shows signs of stress and likely is experiencing some discomfort from punishment and copulation. Nothing serious."

"Then why is she still crying?"

Daneth shrugged. "It could be emotional pain."

"Emotional?"

"Yes. Human females are quite sensitive."

Veck. "So what do we do about that? Nothing?"

He couldn't read Daneth's expression. It had better not be amusement. "I will research now, my lord. I will bring you my recommendations in the morning."

He blew out his breath. "Fine." He knew he sounded peevish. He was often curt, but not usually so irritable. He was becoming as prickly as his little slave.

"Do you wish me to give her an analgesic for pain?"

He hesitated. If her only pain was from punishment, she deserved to feel that. On the other hand, if it was from losing her human maidenhead, he ought to soothe that wound. "Yes."

Daneth produced a needle gun and filled it.

"No." The terror in her voice struck straight through his chest. She rolled against him, cowering.

It shouldn't anger him to see her afraid of Daneth. He hadn't hurt her, at least Zander didn't believe he had. She was foolish—the needle wouldn't hurt, and the drug was only meant to ease her pain. But she didn't trust Daneth. Didn't trust him, either.

"Never mind. She doesn't want it. You may go, Daneth."

"I can take her to sleep in the clinic so the crying doesn't bother you."

The offer was tempting. She'd already taken up so much of his day, and now she threatened to ruin his sleep, too. But she'd tensed beside him as if the idea frightened her.

"No. I believe she's finished. If she continues, I will call you." He gave her a warning glance and swore he saw answering submission in the lowering of her chin.

Daneth left.

"Lights off." Zander rolled on his side to face the human.

"Thank you," she whispered in the dark.

Her human eyes couldn't see him—she blinked in his general direction, but with an unfocused gaze. His eyes worked fine in the dark. It gave him a chance to study her. She looked sweet. Not like the kind of rebellious human who would take a hunk out of his thumb with her teeth.

"Release my wrists...please, my lord?"

He liked her begging. More than he ought to. His horns roughened. "No."

She'd be likely to attempt murder during the night.

She must have expected that answer because she didn't protest. "I need to relieve myself," she said.

"What does that mean?"

Embarrassment colored her skin. "Empty my bladder."

It might be a trick to get her hands free. But then again, she had eaten and drunk not long ago. He commanded her wrists cuffs to release and turned on the light. "The washroom is there, the door in the corner. You have thirty seconds."

She scrambled out of bed and ran to the bathroom door, throwing it open. She didn't bother turning on the light or shutting the door. He heard the sound of her relieving herself and the flush of the waste. She washed and returned, surprising him by holding her wrists back out. He reattached her cuffs to the head of his bed and brushed a lock of her copper hair from her eyes.

She drew in a ragged breath.

Emotional hurt. What in the galactic kingdom did that mean?

"Was the life I took you from so preferable to this one?" His words sounded bitter to his own ears, as if he'd expected her to thank him for buying her and forcing sex until she bore his offspring.

Her green eyes blinked. She had beautiful, long lashes—black as night. "You took me from my mother—the only person in this galaxy who loves me. The only person I love."

Love. The word grated on him. Love was a foolish human construct. Or, if it existed, it mattered far less than humans believed. Had he ever loved? He cast his mind back to his parents. He didn't remember loving them or being loved. All he remembered was the pain of losing them, and the majority of his species, on that horrible day the Finn invaded. He had grieved for them for solar cycles. Was that love?

He fingered one of her curls. It was impossibly soft and silky. He wanted to smell it but not while she watched him with those big green eyes.

Had he given her the same grief he'd felt when he escaped the genocide of the Finn and ended up in Ocretia alone? Not alone—he had the whole pod of devoted Zandians, but no family.

His chest tightened in sympathy for her pain. "Do you want me to return you there?" He didn't know if he would—he couldn't, really, not until he'd bred her. Still, he held his breath for her answer.

She gazed up at him with those lovely eyes, caught in indecision. Her hesitation was enough. He relaxed.

Her eyes filled with tears.

"Why?" he asked, thumbing up the tear that leaked from the corner of her eye and licking it. He loved the taste of her tears almost as much as he disliked her crying. It was a strange paradox.

She closed her eyes and shook her head.

"No, you don't want me to return you there, or, no, you won't tell me why you cry?"

"I...I don't know," she rasped.

He shook his head. *Humans.* If he was smart, he'd get rid of this girl as quickly as possible, before she disrupted his entire pod. He sighed. "How long do humans sleep at one time?"

"They only allowed us five hours at the agrifarm. How long do you sleep? My lord?" She tacked the *my lord* onto the end. The question was still disrespectful, but at least she was starting to learn to speak with deference.

"I sleep four hours. You may rest as long as you like here." The longer, the better—she interrupted too much of his work time as it was.

The corners of her lips lifted in a faint smile. "Thank you, my lord." Her eyes were already drifting closed. He watched her breathing deepen and her muscles relax. She tugged at her wrists in her sleep, her brow furrowing when they didn't move.

She rolled into him, tossing one leg across his hips and making a little cooing sound, like a faint hum.

He smelled his scent on her, her warmth and softness more luxurious than his fine sheets and blankets. His cock hardened again from the contact with her flesh. He ran his fingertip from her bound wrists down her arm and around her small but perky breasts. He traced her nipple. It stiffened and stood up, much like his horns' reaction to her closeness. He had to rub his horns on her. Careful not to disturb her rest, he leaned up on one elbow and dragged one horn down the length of her torso.

She hummed again, her expression blissful. He loved that tiny smile on her. She was far more pleasant when asleep. He rubbed the other horn around her breast, shuddering at the pleasure of it. He wanted to *veck* her again. The first time should have been like this—with her lying face up so he could explore her body and watch her expression.

No, she probably still would've have yelled and bitten him. Hopefully, she'd get used to it soon. When she wasn't testing his temper with her constant sass, he found her intriguing. Far more fascinating than he'd imagined a human female might be. Complex, yes, and deceitful, not unappealing.

He thought about taking her again. It was his right, after all. She was his slave, chained to his bed. But, no, she'd had enough for one day. He didn't want to make her cry again. He'd probably have to do plenty of that again in the next planet rotation.

Chapter Three

She woke alone on Zander's sleeping platform. She opened her eyes without moving, not wanting to call attention to herself. The fabrics touching her skin were silky soft, finely woven with incredibly intricate patterns in beautiful colors—some she'd never seen before.

Zander sat shirtless on his platform in front of his holograms. His back was to her. He worked quickly, fingers flying as he opened holograms and sent them. He had the volume turned low—was that for her? He truly had allowed her to sleep in, as he'd promised. Something warm and syrupy slithered through her chest and belly.

With her gaze, she traced the lines of his rigid muscles from his wide shoulders and down his corded arms, tapering to a narrow waist. Her body heated as she remembered the way he'd taken her the night before, strapped down to the bench with her ass in the air. Something jumped and fluttered in her belly. Her pussy clenched. She squeezed her bottom, testing. It didn't hurt anymore, even though she'd thought she'd die at the time. So the punishment had not been so awful after all. Her pussy still stung, but not in a bad way. It was the initial stretching that had hurt. When he'd entered her the second time, she'd almost enjoyed the feel of him surging inside her. It was like scratching an itch—both satisfying and uncomfortable at the same time. But it had ended sooner than she wanted.

She honestly didn't know why she'd cried afterward. It wasn't because she hurt, although she had. It was more the buildup and shock of the entire day. Being away from familiar surroundings, having to adjust to new rules. Grieving for her mother.

When he'd asked her if she wanted to return to her old life, she hadn't been sure how to answer. She missed her mother, yes. And she'd loved her plants. But her life there had been full of hard work, with little rest or sustenance. Beatings there were brutal—life-threatening. There'd been no beauty.

The punishments here had been painful and humiliating but had caused her no lasting harm. And all she had to do to avoid them was grovel—something she hated, but that only damaged her pride. In Zander's pod, she was surrounded by opulence and beauty. The food and drink practically exploded with flavor. Color and light and fine quality materials glittered at every turn. So far, the worst she had to suffer here was kneeling at Zander's feet, showing him respect, and letting him use her body as often as he pleased. She wondered how often he would please. Daily? More than once a day? That thought should not excite her so much, and she felt guilty for enjoying things here when her mother remained on the agrifarm.

Zander opened a new communication hologram and spoke rapidly in another language to the male whose image appeared in the chamber.

The being raked his eyes over her with a leer and said something.

Zander whipped his head around to look at her and scowled. He waved his hand and disconnected the transmission with a sharp command.

"Cover yourself."

Was he jealous about other males looking at her? The thought shouldn't please her half as much as it did.

"It's a little hard to do with my wrists bound."

His lips tightened.

"Master," she added.

He stood up and walked over, towering over her as he gazed down with a speculative look. "You continue to sass me."

She caught her breath at his glower. Her pussy leaked moisture. Why did his dominance excite her traitorous body?

"I'm sorry." She truly was. She didn't want to start the day off with punishment, not when her dreams had been filled with scenes of the Zandian tracing his fingertips across her breasts and stroking her torso with his horns as if it gave him some kind erotic pleasure.

He shook his head. "I can't believe anything you say, little human. Your deceit is the only constant."

She didn't know how to answer, so she kept still, making her posture and expression subservient, hoping he'd release her wrists so she could use the washroom again.

"Release cuffs."

Blood rushed to her hands and arms. She winced, shaking them out.

Zander still stood above her, staring down. His eyes shone more purple than before, and his hungry expression sent a zing of electricity shooting up her inner thighs, straight to her pussy. She shivered.

His lips twitched and he leaned down and grasped her hips roughly, flipping her over to her belly. She squeezed her eyes closed, thinking he meant to punish her, but he only stroked his large palm over her buttocks.

"Minimal marks. Your buttocks do, indeed, make a good target for punishment."

"How is your thumb?" She didn't dare show her face when she spoke, and it came out in such a tiny voice she thought he didn't hear.

"It's healed." He flipped her back over and held his palm up. "Zandians repair quickly, unlike humans."

She fought the urge to roll her eyes. "May I please use the washroom?"

He stood back. "Go."

And, he dismissed her, turning his back and returning to his work.

She climbed out of bed and jogged to the washroom. It took her a moment to figure out how to illuminate the room and how to shut the door. She used the commode and washed her hands in the sink of polished gray gemstone. The liquid soap smelled of exotic complex spices, earthy and vaguely sweet. She recognized it as part of what made Zander smell so sinful. In the corner stood a cylinder of the same gemstone. Was that where he took the light baths? Remembering the vision she'd had of herself enjoying it, she traced her fingertips along the opening, searching for a spring to open it. Finding the latch, she triggered it, jumping back and gasping when the door lifted vertically rather than in.

Inside shone the same as the outside, a smooth polished stone cylinder.

"You may wash, if you like," Zander called from the other room.

Wash. Was this for washing? She stepped inside and examined the small enclosure. The door slid shut and suddenly water shot out from nozzles all around her.

She yelped. The temperature was warm but the spray hit hard. After she grew accustomed to it, she enjoyed it, but the entire tube filled up fast. Water had reached her waist already, then her chest. She spun in a circle, looking for an off switch. She saw nothing of the kind. Liquid rose to her chin.

"Um...Zander?" Panic pitched her voice higher than usual.

She couldn't hear over the spray of water whether he answered or not.

Oh galaxies, oh suns, oh *veck, veck, veck*. The level reached her nose. She tipped her head back to lift her mouth out of the water and screamed, "Help!"

Water filled the entire cylinder. She held her breath as it rushed in swirls around her, like a mini hurricane. Just when she thought she might die from holding her breath, it began to drain. The tube emptied as quickly as it had filled. She gasped, her heart hammering against her ribs. The door slid open to reveal Zander leaning against the doorframe, amusement playing on his face. And *veeeeck*. The sight of his muscled bare chest sent fresh spirals of arousal straight to her core. Or maybe it was his heavy-lidded gaze.

"Have you never washed in a quick-wash tube before?"

She shook her head, sending droplets flying from the ends of her hair. "No...master."

His lips kicked up another notch. He liked being called that.

Her pussy moistened again.

Zander slid his eyes down the length of her dripping body and back up again, and his irises turned deep violet once more. His horns tilted in her direction.

She craned her neck to peer around the little chamber. "Is there, um, a towel?"

He smirked and hit a control on the side of the cylinder. The door slid shut once more.

"No, wait!" She banged against it. "Please! I don't want another bath."

His deep chuckle echoed against the gemstone walls of the tube.

But, this time, the tube did not fill with water, it filled with warm air, blowing from every direction, drying her body. After a few moments, when her skin had dried, it stopped. Her hair still hung in wet ringlets, but it no longer dripped. The door slid open again.

Zander had gone. Disappointment flickered through her. Wait...was that true? That she missed Zander's mocking presence? Or even his stern one?

She found a large stone comb on the counter. It hadn't been there before, so Zander must've put it there for her. He certainly didn't need a comb with his short hair. She pulled it through her hair and, after investigating the hidden controls on the outer wall, reentered the "quick-wash tube" for a second dry, this time for her hair. She discovered there were also controls for "oil," which sprayed a fine mist of oil over her body. She managed to pull her hair up off her back just in time to avoid getting it sprayed. "Shine" lightly dusted her with the glimmering powder she'd worn on her first day there. Thank the one true star—she'd been afraid Daneth or some other being had washed her before she awoke at Zander's pod, but more likely they'd put her in some form of washtube. Although how did she not drown? She discovered different scents were available—the spicy scent of Zander, and also the lighter, citrusy fragrance she'd smelled on her hair the first day.

She emerged with her long hair dry, a glow on her skin, and smelling fresh and clean. She'd feel incredible if the cuffs on her neck, wrists and ankles didn't rub now that they were wet.

Zander swiveled in his seat when she emerged. Remembering his edict from the day before, she went and knelt at his feet. His usually stern gaze softened and he dropped a hand on the back of her head, stroking her hair. "Yes, if you stay at my feet, you will not be seen while I conduct business." He tweaked a nipple between his thumb and forefinger. "And then you may remain naked, the way I like you."

A shiver of excitement ran through her.

"Forgive me, master." Obviously, it hadn't been her fault she'd been seen—she'd been bound to his bed—but she wanted to experiment with acting slave-like. She liked his amused smile far better than his glower. If winning his approval was truly as easy as feigning subservience, it was worth playing his game.

Or did she actually wish to please him? Surely not.

She did like the way his glittering eyes roved over her.

He hooked a finger through the ring at her collar. His thumb touched the leather. "You washed with these on."

"I cannot remove them, my lord." *Because you hold the controls.*

"Next time, ask me to take them off first. Release wrist cuffs. Release ankle cuffs. Release collar." All five dropped to the floor.

She rubbed the raw skin at her neck.

He wrapped his huge hand around her throat. She caught her breath. One squeeze from that powerful fist would end her life.

"Delicate human skin," he muttered.

Her stomach rumbled, and he released her neck and frowned. "Again?"

She bowed her head, biting back the reminder it had been half a planet's rotation already since she'd eaten. She would be a good slave today. Avoid getting spanked. Learn her way around here.

"Clothe yourself." He jerked his head toward the sleeping platform. While she'd been in the washroom, some being had straightened the covers and left a neat pile of clothing on the end.

She started to stand but saw censure in his expression. She froze. What did he want? Oh. "Yes, my lord." She spoke with her head lowered.

He turned back to his holograms, effectively dismissing her.

Arrogant male.

She stood, her knees cracking from kneeling, and made her way to the sleeping platform. A fluffy pink sweater, knit of the finest natural material she'd ever seen sat on the top of the pile. She picked it up. Downy soft. She rubbed it on her cheeks. She'd never felt anything so soft—not even the fuzzy little seed pods from the *rheebush* she loved so well. It had the same slightly citrus smell as the soap from the washtube. She pulled it over her head. It touched her skin like a caress, hugged her body. For the bottom, there were panties, leggings, and a skirt that was really more like a cape—open in the front and covering the back to mid-thigh. They were also constructed of finely woven fabrics.

Zander's seating platform rotated and he examined her with a critical eye. A frown appeared between his brows.

It shouldn't bother her so much.

"Come here."

She stepped forward to stand before him.

He brushed his thumbs over her nipples, which stood out under the fabric. His touch hardened them, pushing them forward even more. One of them poked through the open weave.

"No." His voice was harsh. "This is not acceptable."

She covered her breasts with her hands, a flush of heat climbing her neck to her face.

He flicked open a hologram and barked something in his own language to a servant. She hadn't considered the Zandians spoke another language. Every being had been speaking Ocretion, the language of the planet they were on. The galaxy superpower who had overtaken Earth and stripped all her resources, including humans, one thousand solar cycles before.

He pointed once more at his feet. "Kneel."

She dropped to her knees, and he went back to work. A few moments later, an older Zandian came in carrying a stack of clothing. He set it on the bed and fished a tiny undershirt out of the pile. "Will this do, my lord?"

Zander spared a glance over his shoulder. "Yes."

"Will that be all, my lord?"

"Yes. You are dismissed."

"Thank you, my lord."

The elderly Zandian bowed and backed out of the room.

She started to move but realized she should wait for his direction. She raised her eyes, expectantly.

He glanced down, his mouth open like he was about to bark something. He halted and stared. "I like that look on you."

She glanced down at the clothing.

"Not the clothing. Your face."

A flush of heat warmed her cheeks and ears. What expression had she worn—supplication? Of course the arrogant bastard liked that. Her annoyance didn't travel to her sex, however, which clenched at the thought. Holy star, why? Her pussy liked subservience? Or liked that he liked it? Or was it the way his eyes bore into her, shining a deep, hungry amethyst?

Maybe she was crazy or perhaps it was some strange survival instinct finally kicking in, but she *wanted* his desire. Not only because it was better than his cold, impatient indifference.

He reached down and grasped the hem of her sweater, pulling it over her head and staring at her breasts like she hadn't already been naked for him for the entire past planet rotation. His nostrils flared.

Something on his hologram flashed and he blinked several times, shaking out of it. He jerked his head toward the clothing on the bed. "Dress yourself. No nipples showing. Gunt will take you to the kitchen to dine." Dismissed, like the elderly servant.

She stood and he handed her the pink sweater. The undershirt was constructed of the finest material—some kind of spider silk. It slid along her skin in glorious sensations—a creation of true beauty and function. The pink sweater fit back over the top. She wished Zander had a mirror or self-imager in his chamber. She felt so beautiful.

"Gunt," Zander called out.

The door to his chamber slid open and the guard who stood there stepped in. "Yes, my lord?"

"Escort Lamira to the kitchen."

"Yes, my lord."

Zander didn't spare a glance for her, which shouldn't have been so disappointing.

When the door shut, Gunt took her elbow. An unpleasant jolt ran through her. It settled in the pit of her stomach. "So, he let you wear clothes today?" His lips curled in a sneer.

Her chest tightened. "Yes."

Obviously. What else did he want her to say? He was drawing her into a complaint against Zander, she supposed. She'd have to watch out for him.

He led her down the colorful hallway. Expensive rugs caressed her bare feet. "What's it like being the prince's sex slave?"

Two disparate things happened. One, her pussy moistened and clenched at hearing herself called Zander's sex slave. Two, her fingers curled into a fist because she wanted to punch the sleazy Zandian guard.

She chose not to answer.

"That bad, huh? I figured when I saw your bare ass shredded yesterday. He's a harsh master. Where'd you come from?"

Was this considered polite conversation? She didn't care for the guard or his questions.

She paused to show she wasn't interested in the conversation, but long enough to imply she had completely snubbed him. "I worked on an agrifarm." She didn't know if Zander's guards were allowed to beat her, too, but she didn't want to take the chance. Thankfully, they'd arrived at the kitchen.

The chef, Barr, laid out three dishes of food on the counter.

"Good morning, Master Barr," she said brightly. If she was going to be staying here, it was time she started cultivating some friends. Especially the ones who fed her.

Gunt, her guard, scowled.

Barr's skin turned more violet, and his horns twisted. His eyes traveled down to her breasts, even though she wore clothing today. "Lovely sweater, my lady, er, Lamira."

"Thank you." Her stomach rumbled. "Is this food for me?"

"Yes, my l—" He stopped himself short. "Yes. Either a citrus-flavored breakfast pudding, shredded leg of maca, or—"

"The pudding sounds amazing." She didn't think her stomach could handle the meat plates first thing in the morning.

Barr pushed the bowl to her.

She picked up the gleaming spoon, which must be made of some precious metal because it felt smooth and heavy in her hand. She took a bite.

And nearly convulsed with pleasure. Her eyes might have rolled back in her head.

"Mmm," she rumbled, swirling the creamy, rich treat around in her mouth. "This is incredible, Master Barr."

"Just Barr. We're equals, remember?" His eyes crinkled and he bobbed his head.

"Thank you, this is so delicious." She took another bite and once more rolled her eyes heavenward as she turned it around in her mouth.

"I could send the food to the prince's chambers for you next time. If you wish."

She flashed him a smile. "Thank you, that's very kind of you. It's nice for me to get out, though. And I have a feeling Prince Zander was happy to be rid of me for a short time, as well."

"Oh, I doubt that," Barr said.

Gunt's upper lip curled.

"No, I think he's a busy being, and my presence has disrupted his routine. He gets annoyed with me."

Barr reached out as if to pat her hand then withdrew his to his side. "I'm sure you'll settle in soon. We are all happy he has chosen...er, to breed." Barr's skin turned a pinky-purple.

She suspected he was right about her settling in soon and she wasn't sure how she felt about it. Part of her wanted to keep rebelling, to fight her new role here, to reject this "sex slave/breeder" identity. But her body had accepted it from the moment he took her virginity. Her spirit may be softening to it, too. Here she was, making friends in the kitchen. She would learn her way around the pod. Things were beautiful here. The food was worth killing for. And Zander...

Her pussy clenched again at the memory of her huge, muscle-bound master, his thick cock stretching her wide while he pounded into her. She might get used to that. Her tummy fluttered. She might learn to please him and avoid his punishments.

She finished the pudding and stood, giving her spoon one last lick. "Thank you so much, Barr. If I only had that to eat for the rest of my life, I would die a happy woman."

He chuckled and took the bowl away, his skin flushing violet again.

Gunt gripped her elbow. "Let's go, slave."

Barr frowned. "The prince said to call her *Lamira*. That she serves him like we do."

Gunt shrugged. "Let's go, Lamira."

She flashed Barr a grateful smile over her shoulder. At least there was one being in this pod who liked her.

Once in the hallway, Gunt stopped. "Do you want a tour? Of the whole pod?"

It was too good an offer to turn down, even if she disliked Gunt. "Yes, please."

He led her down the hall in the opposite direction from Zander's chamber. Like her first day, she noticed how beautiful even the corridors were. The walls were plastered in beautiful hues and natural light— she stopped and looked up. How did they get so much natural light in there? Ocretia's atmosphere was covered in smog. Normally, the three suns did not offer so much light.

A giant crystal was embedded in a skylight in the ceiling above. Its crystalline structure magnified the light coming in. Was this what he meant when he spoke of light baths?

"Whoa."

"The crystals are all from Zandia. They provide our species with energy. They're also used in laser weaponry, which is why the Finn invaded our planet—to control the supply."

Gunt pilfered crystals from Zander and sold them on the black market.

The knowing dropped into her head from nowhere. Things she shouldn't know arrived in her head without any deductive reasoning. Without being told.

She hadn't liked the male, but she couldn't tell Zander. Not without revealing the trait that would equate to certain death. Humans with gifts like hers were executed. Zander would be required to turn her over to the Ocretion law for disposal.

He opened a door into a huge open room with vaulted ceilings and even more light. The longest table she'd ever seen took up much of the floor. Embedded like skylights glittered five giant crystals—each twice the size of her head. The light pouring in wasn't only magnified sunrays—the crystals cast rainbows around the room. She gasped.

She could grow things in here. Wonderful food and flowers.

"The formal dining room." He pulled her back and shut the door, continuing down the corridor. "The great hall." Another enormous room, with a domed ceiling and a giant crystal beaming light down. A large, stone chair sat upon a dais. "This is where Prince Zander hears the complaints, requests, and cases of our species."

"How many Zandians are there?" From what she'd heard, the majority had been wiped out by the Finns when they invaded the planet.

"Very few. Two hundred. Maybe three. They're scattered about, but many come to visit this pod for the crystal light baths. They are open to any Zandian, one planet rotation a week. The same day Prince Zander hears cases and pleas from our species."

He tugged her elbow, pulling her from the beautiful room, and led her down a narrow hall with lower ceilings. "This is the staff quarters." Even though they were not as magnificent as the rest of the pod, they were still beautiful to her.

"This is my chamber." He stopped and opened the door, pushing her forward, as if to guide her in.

She froze, catching his intent. "I should get back to Prince Zander."

He swiveled his dark-violet gaze to her. "You're the only female we've had around here in a long time. We've never had one live here."

She tried to back up. "Well, I'm just a human—hardly pleasing to your species, if Lord Zander can be believed."

Gunt's eyes glittered. "Oh, I think every male in the pod finds you pleasing." He pushed her against the doorframe, pressing his large body against her, mashing her back into the hard wood frame.

She threw her hands up to push him back, but he was too solid.

"I could help you around here. Protect you from the rest of them." He leaned forward, his horns pulsing, his breath foul in her face. "Maybe even help you escape."

"Oh sure. And all I have to do is what? Suck your cock?"

Zandians didn't understand sarcasm. Gunt's eyes turned dark-purple. "Not *all*. But, yes. That's a start."

She turned her cheek away from him. "No thanks."

Gunt's expression changed in slow motion, developing from lust to rage. His hand shot out and closed around her throat. "What?"

She gurgled, trying to suck air through her closed windpipe.

"You think you're too good for me, *vecking* human?"

She shook her head, and he dropped her. A door whisked open down the hall. Before he had the opportunity to do or say anything more, she took off running. The expensive rugs slipped under her bare feet. She didn't hear Gunt's footsteps behind her. Chancing a look back, she saw him walking purposefully but not running. Perfecting his cover, she supposed, in case anyone saw them.

She slowed her steps as well. No reason she should act guilty either. By the time she reached Zander's door, she'd caught her breath and held her head high. She didn't know how to open it, though. She stared at the door, waiting for Gunt.

He arrived behind her. "Let me know when you change your mind," he said as he reached past her, pressed his palm to the security screen, and opened the door. "If you tell the prince, I'll say you offered yourself to me. He won't believe a human over his own species."

Chapter Four

"She'll be back from her feeding soon," Zander told Daneth, who had arrived full of information on human reproduction. "You can take her for the implants then."

Daneth believed a "natural conception" was important for Zander's child. He said they would only resort to harvesting her eggs and breeding offspring in the lab if natural conception failed after 200 planet rotations. Zander had grumbled about having to breed the human for two hundred days and nights. If things went as badly as they had the night before, he would insist on a lab breeding by the third moon passing.

Lamira burst into his chamber, a spot of high color on her cheeks. Red blotches marred the slender column of her neck, too. It must be from the wet collar.

Humans and their weak constitution.

"What took you so long?"

She lifted a shaky hand to her hair and smoothed it away from her face. "Oh...um, Gunt gave me a tour of the pod." She pulled her shoulders back and drew a breath. "My lord, the crystals provide excellent light here. I could grow plants for the pod—food you could eat, or flowers."

"I have no need for—"

Daneth lifted a finger. "My lord, this could be useful knowledge for rebuilding an over-mined planet."

He was right. But surely that wasn't the only reason this human had been selected as his best mate. Knowledge of agriculture could be found or bought. "All right," he grumbled. "You may grow things, Lamira. Later, you can tell me what supplies you'll need."

Her face lit up so bright, it almost made the hassle worth it. Almost.

"You may take her now."

Daneth planned to insert sensors in her female canal and womb which would send constant feedback of her physical state directly to Zander's armband.

Lamira's eyes went wide, the beautiful green of her irises growing as her pupils shrank. He didn't have to be an expert on humans to recognize fear. *Veck*, he could smell it on her. Why was she so afraid of Daneth?

Before he could explain what would happen to her, Daneth had touched his wand to the back of her neck, and she crumpled. His physician swung her up over his shoulder.

"Not like that," he snapped.

Daneth put her down, supporting her upright, and stared at him.

"Don't carry her like that. It's disrespectful to the mother of my future children."

Daneth bowed. "Yes, of course, my lord. You're quite right." He picked her up in two arms, cradled like a baby, instead.

Zander scowled, not liking the intimacy of it. "I will carry her." He waved an impatient hand to dismantle the hologram he'd been working on and surged to his feet, snatching his bride—no. Not his bride—his slave—from Daneth's grasp. "Let's go," he growled.

"The procedure will only take a few moments, my lord. It would be useful if you stayed, and I could show you what I learned about her anatomy and arousal."

His guard Gunt followed them with an overly-interested gaze. Zander turned back to give a disapproving glare.

To Daneth, he said, "If you insist."

"I would not presume to do so, my lord."

That wasn't true. Daneth presumed to insist on a great many things, but he let it go.

In the lab, he laid Lamira on Daneth's table and helped the physician strip off her clothing. Daneth attached new ankle and wrist cuffs to her. He clipped her two wrists together over her head and attached her ankles to a pair of stirrups that lifted and spread her knees wide. With an imagescope, he implanted several miniscule sensors inside her vaginal and uterine walls.

He requested Zander's armband and programmed the sensors to transmit directly to it.

"Now, my lord, let me show you what I learned. The human female's climax is important for breeding. The contraction of her vaginal and uterine muscles help propel your seed up into her cervix. Deep penetration would be important if she were breeding with another human, but, considering your size, it should not be an issue."

His little human stirred, the effects of the stunning wearing off.

"Ah, good timing. As soon as all her faculties return, we can test it out. In the meantime, let's examine her anatomy." He peeled back Lamira's labia, exposing the heart of her vagina. With one thumb, he lifted a hood of flesh, revealing a delicate pink button.

Zander gritted his teeth, not liking Daneth touching her.

"This is called the clitoris. Touching it gives her pleasure. See?"

The little nub had thickened as Daneth brushed his thumb over it.

It took all his control not to shove the male aside. "I'll do it," he clipped.

"Of course, my lord."

Lamira's lids fluttered open and she stared at him with those spectacular green eyes. Green with gold starbursts.

He took Daneth's place between her legs, fumbling to find the secret nubbin.

Lamira cried out when he touched it, yanking against her cuffs and giving him an accusatory look—half panicked, half something else.

He hesitated. Had he been too rough?

"She likes it. Look at her responses." Daneth kept his voice low, as if Lamira might not hear him. He wasn't sure what responses the male meant until Daneth pointed at the projection from his wristband.

Thirty percent aroused.

Interesting. So that was what aroused looked like. Angry and panicked.

He slid his thumb over the nubbin in a slow circle.

Her face flushed and her breath shortened. She swallowed. Her inner thighs began to quiver.

"Now, inside her channel is another cluster of nerve endings that give her pleasure. It can be found with your finger on the front wall if you reach in and make this motion." Daneth curled two fingers as if beckoning someone. "You will find a place where the tissue tightens when touched, the same way her nipples do." Daneth reached out to tweak one of her nipples but stopped shy of it, probably catching Zander's murderous glare.

Lamira thrashed against the bonds holding her wrists, trying to move away from the physician.

"Ahem." Daneth cleared his throat and took a step back. "Why don't you attempt to inseminate her now, my lord, and we can monitor her arousal rate?"

His cock had no arguments with that plan, already straining against his pants, painfully thick. Zandian moons, he'd been ready to mount her again since the moment he woke up that morning.

He released his cock.

"No." Lamira thrashed her head from side to side. "No, you are *not* going to breed me here like this."

Veck. Her resistance again. It took some of the eagerness right out of his spear. But the breeding had to be done. The sooner she conceived, the sooner he could stop torturing the poor girl. Although that plan didn't ring true on several levels.

The table was the wrong height for him to enter her. Plus, he preferred the sight of her ass, so lush, soft and feminine. He unbuckled one of her ankles from the stirrup. The moment her foot came free, she kicked him in the nose, hard.

"Ack!" Stars flashed before his eyes. "Enough, human," he roared. "I am tired of your resistance."

When his vision cleared, he found her cowering, as best as someone with three limbs cuffed can cower. Her one free leg was tucked up and she'd twisted in a protective manner. Mostly it was the terror on her face that inspired his sympathy and calmed his ire.

~.~

She hadn't meant to kick him in the face. She'd only wanted to get free of the bonds. The last thing she wanted was to have sex with Zander while his scientist or physician or whatever Daneth was watched.

But she'd hit Zander square in the nose, and a trickle of red-violet blood ran from his nostril n.

"I'm sorry, I didn't mean to—"

Zander swiped at the blood with the back of his hand. With verbal command, he released the cuff on her other ankle and both wrists.

She tried to draw up into a ball, but he grabbed both ankles and pulled her off the table.

He flipped her around and shoved her upper body over the examination table, pulling her wrists behind her back and clipping them together.

She tensed, knowing what was sure to come next.

"I'm sorry," she moaned, knowing it wouldn't do any good.

"I believe you're sorry." To her surprise, it sounded like Zander had recovered his temper. It didn't stop him from clapping his huge hand down across her buttocks.

She lurched forward, as if she might somehow get away, but he continued to spank her, his large, paddle-like hand crashing down on her upturned buttocks again and again.

"Ow, please," she moaned. She'd given up on defiance, at least for the moment. A little sympathy wouldn't hurt right now.

Zander continued to light a fire on her behind, his huge hand clapping down on one cheek then the other then right in the middle.

"Look at her arousal rate," Daneth murmured.

Arousal rate?

She must've heard wrong. Her ass was on fire. She was completely humiliated, being punished in front of Daneth and now—

Zander ran a finger across her already engorged clit. It pulsed and her pussy clenched.

Okay, her pussy might be a little wet. Actually, dripping wet. But that didn't mean she was aroused, did it? Aroused by the spanking? Or what had happened before?

It didn't matter because Zander's malehood prodded her entrance and, for some reason, she pushed back at him, as if she wanted his entry.

The head of his cock stretched her wide, and he eased into her.

She caught her breath, but it didn't hurt this time. Not at all. In fact, it felt...

Delicious.

A wanton sort of sound escaped her lips.

Zander gripped her elbows, using the bound circle of her arms to brace her each time he shoved deep inside.

"Zander," she gasped.

A growling sound came from his throat.

She arched back for him, spread her legs wider as he stroked in and out, his giant cock filling her with each plunge.

"Zander," she cried again, sounding a bit more desperate.

"Nearing orgasm," Daneth's cool manicured voice didn't take her out of the moment. She heard it, as if in the distance, far away from the only beings that mattered—Zander and her.

Zander released her arms and gripped her pelvis with one hand, reaching around the front of it with the other. He rubbed his finger over her clitoris, and she shrieked.

"Oh please, oh—"

"Zandian moons, yes." Zander shoved deep inside her, his hot seed filling her.

Flickering lights danced before her eyes, and she let go. Her muscles spasmed around his cock, squeezing around his thick girth. They continued clenching, ripples of release that went on and on, even after Zander started to pull out.

"Wait—do you feel how her orgasm milks your seed up higher in her channel?"

Zander pushed back inside her.

"It serves an important purpose for conception."

She shivered. Hearing her physical processes discussed made them all the more intense. Her internal muscles continued contracting strongly around his cock.

"Now, we want to invert her so she doesn't lose any of your seed."

Zander flipped her up into his arms, cradled like a baby, but with her ass-end slightly higher than her head.

She ducked her face into his shoulder, not wanting to show it after—well, after any of it.

"She should rest like that for at least a half hour. I can chain her up here or—"

"No."

She was relieved at how quickly Zander cut in.

"I'll take her back to my chamber. Give me something with which to cover her."

Daneth produced a thin blanket, which Zander wrapped around her.

She felt oddly like a baby. It wasn't an unpleasant sensation.

Zander carried her out of the examination room and back to his chamber.

Gunt, the odious guard, watched with his lip curled as they passed him at the door. It made her stomach tighten. She wondered if she ought to tell Zander—not about what Gunt had done to her, but about the crystals he was stealing. No—what was she thinking? She couldn't. How would she explain her knowledge?

Zander carried her into his chamber. She expected him to lay her on the bed, perhaps with orders to keep her butt in the air, but instead he sat upon his sleep disk and continued to hold her, cradled in his arms. He tossed the blanket off and studied her, his violet eyes sweeping the length of her body, lingering on her breasts then her face.

She gazed up at him. Like with the bite mark, his nose had already healed. "I truly didn't mean to kick you in the face."

"Hush." He picked up one of her curls and twirled it around a finger.

For once, she did as he asked and stopped speaking. After all the shock of the past few days, being held by him eased the strain. No, it more than eased the strain—it felt incredible. She didn't want to say or do anything to bring it to a close.

Zander seemed softened by sex, his features relaxed, his touch gentle. He traced one of her eyebrows with the pad of his finger, measured the size of her ear with his digits, and compared it to his own, as if fascinated by her. He slid her upper body off onto the bed, keeping her pelvis in his lap with her legs in the air, and explored the intimate folds of her sex. His horns thickened, and they leaned toward her.

This time, she didn't mind the scientific curiosity, as Zander parted her lips and, once more, found her clit. He didn't seem intent on arousing her. Instead, his touch was exploratory. He brushed her clit with a feather-like touch, fingered her labia.

It brought her pleasure, but not in a needy way, like before. This time, she found it profoundly relaxing. Her eyes drifted closed and she floated away as Zander continued his light caresses and explored every part of her.

Being his slave might have some perks. No, she shouldn't think this way. Guilt stabbed her conscience. She couldn't be happy here with her mother all alone at the agrifarm.

~.~

Zander couldn't believe how delicate her parts were compared to his. Sweet little ears, a button nose, the light dusting of coppery freckles across her glowing skin. Her flesh was so soft, and he loved the way she smelled—like fresh, delicious female mixed with his own scent.

He rubbed his horns along her inner thighs and her flat belly, nudged them against her clitoris. He held her for far longer than he should—he had twenty other things to do—but the more relaxed and contented she appeared to grow in his arms, the less he wanted to put her down. But Daneth had said thirty minutes and it had already been forty-five. He eased her down onto the bed and extricated himself.

"I have work to do. You are free to rest."

She gave him a slow blink, as if she'd drifted far away, and it took her a moment to understand him. Then she sat up, propped on one hand, and watched him as he resumed his position at his work wall. He flipped on the latest charts from his trades that day.

"My lord?"

He gritted his teeth at the interruption. "What?"

"May I use the washroom?"

"You don't have to ask me things like that," he snapped, but instantly regretted it, because the peace slid away from her expression, replaced with that familiar look of stubborn pride.

She lifted her chin. "Forgive me for trying to learn my place."

Another lie. Humans called it something. That's right, *sarcasm*. He turned back to his work again and she went to the washroom.

It occurred to him that she might be rinsing out his seed. Was that possible? He certainly wouldn't put it past the deceitful little human.

When she returned, he beckoned her to him. "Come, Lamira."

She hesitated but pleased him by obeying.

He'd intended to be stern and stand her before him for questioning, but his hands reached of their own accord and pulled her onto his lap.

Well.

He did like the feel of her on his thighs. So light and soft in his arms. So easy to control. He enjoyed the weight of her, small and helpless, yielding, for now. His.

It gave him a good vantage point for studying her face while reminding her who she belonged to.

"Lamira, you will not be permitted to wash out my seed."

She blinked at him. He didn't know her well enough yet to know if it was faked, or not. "You think I washed out your seed?" Her lip curled a little and he saw the flash of anger in her face.

Her bare breasts were so close to him, he forgot himself and palmed one.

He expected her to fight him—to wince and twist away, but confusion flitted across her face and, to his surprise, she rocked on his lap, arching her breast into his hand, as if she liked his touch.

"I would punish you if you did." His voice sounded deeper than usual. His wristband flashed something at him—her readouts.

Forty percent arousal.

In truth? From what? The breast squeeze?

He slid his hand between her knees, stroking up her inner thigh.

Her breath quickened.

He reached her pussy, still swollen from their breeding. With his middle finger, he stroked along her slit, prodding at the opening.

Sixty percent aroused.

"Did you?" His voice definitely sounded hoarse.

She flinched when he entered her, but the mewl from her lips sounded wanton.

"Are you sore?"

"Yes...a little. But I...don't mind it."

The shock of her admission flamed his passion, which had already renewed in full force. But he couldn't breed with the little human again. She'd just told him she was sore.

"You don't mind? But why did you kick me in the face, then?"

She stiffened, and he wished he hadn't brought it up, although he probably did owe her a more substantial punishment for it. Her full arousal during the spanking had redirected his attention at the time.

She clenched her teeth. "I don't wish to be inspected and bred like an animal. It's humiliating to have Daneth watching while you—" Her eyes swam with tears.

"I see."

For once, he believed her. She may be a slave, but she still had pride. He should not underestimate it. She'd found Daneth's presence humiliating. Perhaps that was why she hated to go with him—not because he'd hurt her, but because he embarrassed her.

He slid his finger inside her, not to be certain she hadn't washed—he believed she hadn't—but because he wanted to feel her wet heat all over again. It had only been an hour since he'd had her, but he wanted her again.

She gasped and clutched at his shirt with her bound hands.

Eighty-three percent aroused.

"You are my breeder," he said, pushing his finger all the way inside her, pumping it a few times. "If my physician needs to be present to monitor things, you will have to adjust."

He added a second finger.

Eighty-nine percent aroused.

"Or you'll be punished."

Ninety-four percent aroused.

Had the threat of punishment bumped up her arousal rate? She'd become 100 percent aroused during her spanking earlier.

"Why does punishment arouse you?"

Her tissues literally plumped against his fingers, growing more swollen and slick,

One hundred percent aroused.

She rocked her pelvis to meet his thrusting fingers. Her head fell back and to the side, her lovely copper hair falling across her bare shoulder and breast.

"It doesn't."

Another lie.

He picked her up by the waist and spun her around to face away from him, her legs wide and hooked outside his knees. He delivered a sharp slap to her pussy.

The *fully aroused* message blinked in red in his left peripheral vision.

He slapped her again. "I've lost all patience with your lies."

"Oh because you were *full* of patience before."

Her words gave him pause, because they were not true, and then he recognize them as the annoying human communication habit—*sarcasm.*

He slapped harder.

She cried out and covered her mons with both bound hands.

He picked up her wrists and clipped them together behind his head, which had the pleasing effect of lifting her breasts. He squeezed both her nipples at the same time, pinching hard enough to make her squirm.

He shouldn't enjoy hurting her. Except it excited her, too. Her nipples were hard as little pebbles; the scent of her fresh arousal filled the room. With the fingers of one hand, he continued pinching and rolling her nipple, while the digits of the other once more sought her hot core.

This time, when they penetrated her, there was no mistaking the wanton tone in her moan.

"Do I need to breed you again to teach you who you belong to?"

She bowed up, arching her pelvis and rocking his fingers into her tight channel.

Fully aroused kept blinking.

Veck it. She deserved a little more pain.

He deserved a little more pleasure for putting up with such a naughty slave.

He reached between their bodies to free his length, lifted her hips, and speared her with his malehood.

"Oh." Just one syllable, but the little cry nearly drove him wild.

He mastered her easily, lifting and lowering her onto his shaft, marveling at the way her perky breasts bobbed up and down with the movement.

"Is this what you need, my naughty little slave?"

"Ohh..."

Her hands were still trapped behind his head and she used them now, gripping his head and leveraging her hips over his cock.

She felt so good, her tight wet pussy squeezing his cock like a glove. He didn't want it ever to end. But his little human was sore. Plus, the need to drive into her more deeply gripped him. He lifted her from his lap and carried her to the sleep disk, tossing her onto her back.

He shoved his pants off. To his surprise, when he crawled over her, she brought her bound hands to the hem of his shirt, tugging it up over his abs. He helped her, flinging his shirt off.

She spread her knees for him when he crawled up, and her surrender nearly took his breath away. Her long coppery waves fanned out around her face, the striking green eyes flashed dark with desire.

Desire? Truly? From his little human?

His own lust spiked even higher and he had to hold back to keep from tearing her apart.

Fragile human.

He forced his breath to slow, somehow kept from shoving into her with all the force he wanted to unleash.

She winced and he almost stopped, but her legs wrapped around his back and she pulled him in closer.

She wanted it this time.

His beautiful little human slave.

He pumped into her with measured strokes, holding back with great effort.

Her eyes rolled back, she arched underneath him. "My lord..." she moaned.

All moons of Zander, she shattered his control. He drove deep, angling for the pleasure place Daneth had described. Her channel practically gushed moisture, the slickness allowing him to plow even deeper, stretching her wide to take his girth.

She moaned and rolled her head, her bound hands reaching for him.

He forced them over her head and pinned them there as he rode her. Rational thought left him. A primitive, driving force took over. He found a hard, pounding rhythm, and she matched it, lifting her hips to receive him on each instroke.

Little cries left her lips. He'd never seen anything so beautiful. He bent his head and bit her shoulder, her neck, her ear, all the while sawing in and out of her with vicious thrusts.

"Zander..."

The sound of his name on her lips made him bury himself deep inside her and come—hot ribbons of his seed filling her channel a second time.

Too late, he remembered to watch and wait for her orgasm, but it didn't matter because the squeezing of her muscles told him she'd reached it before his eyes found the readouts.

Her climax was *vecking* glorious. Her mouth opened into a perfect O, her breasts thrust up as she arched, lifting her bottom to meet him, pushing back with more strength than he'd thought she possessed. When it passed, she collapsed, suddenly limp. Her cheeks were flushed a charming shade of pink, her eyes bright and glassy. She panted to regain her breath.

Yes, he could see the appeal of a human slave. He hadn't understood it before, but now, with one glistening underneath him, he saw what he'd been missing. He would have to be careful she didn't become too big a distraction. And stay on his toes, because he couldn't trust anything that came out of her mouth.

~.~

For the second time, Zander settled on the sleeping platform. He scooted the lower half of her over his lap, to raise her hips, her legs lifted up along his torso. She hadn't expected him to breed her again. Hadn't expected her own reaction to it. Her body had responded to the Zandian prince as if it belonged to someone else's brain. From the moment he pulled her onto his lap, flames of desire had licked her into a frenzy.

And *veck*, yes. He had delivered. He'd found all her pleasure zones. He'd been rough—too rough. She'd be sore in more than one place, but she didn't mind one bit. The euphoria flowing through her now made her wonder what her objection to being Zander's sex slave had been in the first place. Apart from missing her mother, her life had improved five hundred times over.

Zander stroked his large palm down her thigh, his touch light as a caress. He bent his head and rubbed her calf with one of his horns. It tickled.

"You *are* lovely."

He put the emphasis on *are,* as if someone—like himself—had argued she wasn't.

She decided staying silent was best, since there was no good answer to a backwards compliment like that.

"You were a good little slave, taking my cock again so soon."

His words should not affect her the way they did, but as if he'd spoken some tremendous endearment, warmth swirled in her chest, turning her insides gooey with a desire to please. To please? That wasn't her. That had never been her.

Of course, she'd never had sex before—particularly not with a hot Zandian.

He brought his thumb to her slit and stroked straight up to her clitoris again, rubbing lightly. "A good little slave to orgasm as soon as I finish."

Frissons of heat traveled down her inner thighs, incited by his touch. Her belly quivered. "Please no more," she whimpered, not because it hurt, but because she didn't think she could take any more orgasms. It was all too intense.

"I won't," he murmured.

He thought she meant no more breeding. He continued to stroke her.

Her heart rate, which had finally slowed after her climax, now climbed in speed again. "Zander," she choked.

His eyes flicked to his cuff and something he saw there explained her predicament. "Ah." His lips curled into a satisfied smile. "I see. My touch has excited you again." His thumb stopped moving but remained on her stiffened bud.

"How many times can a human female orgasm?" It sounded more like rhetorical musing than a real question.

"No." She shook her head. "No more, please."

He flashed a wicked grin. "No more breeding. Just another orgasm. To pull my seed up higher."

She struggled to comprehend his meaning. Before she arrived at any possible conclusion, he palmed her ass with both hands and lifted, bringing her pussy right to his mouth.

She shrieked when his tongue licked into her—more from the shock of pleasure than from any real resistance.

He sucked her pleasure center, licked along the insides of her labia, penetrated her with his tongue.

Her face grew hot, her breath short. She clamped her knees around his ears. When one of her calves brushed his horn, he groaned.

Were they sensitive?

She deliberately rubbed both horns with her lower legs.

His fingers dug into her ass; his tongue lashed her pussy, He pulled her up and down over his mouth.

A scream rose in her throat.

She kicked and thrashed with her legs—not to push him away, only desperate for relief.

He shifted one of his hands under her ass, bringing his thumb to her anus.

She came, hard, bucking in his hands, as he wrung a third orgasm out of her.

"Good girl," he murmured.

Once more, the praise warmed her.

He eased her back down to his lap and pushed her knees open like butterfly wings. "Show me this little pussy of yours. I'm beginning to grow quite fond of it."

Her head swam. No, those were not words to swoon over.

He pulled the cheeks of her ass apart and inspected her anus. "I'm going to take you there, too. It will hurt, I suppose, because you're so tiny. I'll reserve it for punishment."

Her pussy clenched and he noticed.

"You like when I talk about punishment."

She shook her head. "No, I don't."

He flashed the cuff in her direction. "I have proof. And that's another lie. I'm going to start punishing you for lies. Perhaps your first punishment will be me taking your ass."

Her mouth went dry. She attempted to squeeze her bottom together, but it was impossible with him holding her cheeks spread wide. "No, my lord, Please."

His lips curved into a smile; his eyes grew heavy-lidded. "Not this time. But you've been warned."

Her pussy clenched again.

Mother Earth, her core should not be a quivering, bundle of heated nerves right now. Why did his threats affect her that way?

He sighed. "All right, little slave. You've taken me from my work all day. Now it's time for me to put you to work."

"I thought this was my work."

His mouth stretched into a toothy smile. "You're right, it is. But now you're going to make me your list of supplies for the plants you want to grow here. I'll have them delivered tomorrow."

He lifted her from his lap and crawled off the platform, pulling his clothes back on.

Hooking a finger in the ring in her collar, he tugged gently, forcing her to crawl to the edge. "Come." He lifted her off the sleeping platform and onto her feet. Using the collar once more, he led her to his work station and pointed at his feet. "Kneel."

A 3D hologram popped up with a picture of a memo pad and a pen.

She'd never used the technology before—communications and information systems were forbidden to slaves. The very fact she could read was a secret she kept as hidden as her claircognizance. But Zander didn't seem to know it was forbidden, and her pride kept her from playing dumb. She reached for the virtual pen and twirled it in the air, watching as the letters scrawled on the pad.

As she built her list, her spirits rose. But she shouldn't be happy about being an alien's sex slave. Her father would roll over in his grave. He didn't die trying to liberate humans to have his daughter drop to her knees and happily serve the first master who gave her an orgasm.

Chapter Five

Zander rubbed his horns against Lamira's bare back. She lay naked in bed beside him, her wrists cuffed to the bed, one knee drawn up in sleep.

"Mmm." She stirred, rolling toward him as much as the cuffs allowed.

"Disconnect cuffs."

Her wrists came free, and she turned to face him, blinking her beautiful wide-set eyes.

He loved having her in his sleepdisk. Loved waking with her soft, naked form ready and willing beside him. Today was the day he made himself available to his people, but there was probably still time to enjoy his slave's lush body.

"Do you need to use the washroom?" He'd begun to understand her physical needs.

"Yes, please." She rolled off the bed and darted to take care of her needs.

He stretched onto his back and stroked his throbbing cock.

When Lamira emerged, she eyed his cock. "If I were trained as a sex slave, what would I know how to do?"

He smirked. "Are you asking me to train you?"

He expected her to scowl, but she shrugged, the corners of her mouth turning up. "I guess I'm wondering why they would need any training at all if they're bound and used at will." There was a new quality to her voice he didn't recognize. Was it teasing?

"Come here and I'll give you your first lesson, slave girl."

He'd guessed right, because she smiled in reply and crawled up over him her lids lowered seductively.

Lust kicked through him, making his cock surge in his fist. "Put your arms behind your back." When she did, he ordered, "Connect cuffs."

She gave an exaggerated scowl. More teasing, he suspected. Or playing of some sort. Another form of human dishonesty. Funny how it didn't bother him so much this morning. Maybe he was getting used to her.

He angled his cock toward her face. "Put your mouth over it."

Her jaw went slack and eyes widened.

"Be a good slave or you'll go over my knee for a spanking."

That excited her. He no longer needed to watch the flash of her arousal rate from his cuff—he was learning her physical signs. The way her pupils dilated, her breath quickened. Sometimes she blushed—he loved that.

She licked her lips and bent at the waist. "Like this?" she whispered when her lips reached his cock.

A drop of opalescent pre-cum shimmered. Her tongue darted out and she tasted it.

He bit back a groan. He couldn't imagine any scene sexier than the one unfolding now. "Take it," he growled.

She obediently parted her lips and lowered her head over his cock, enveloping it in the hot, moist recess of her mouth.

"Lamira," he rasped and wrapped a fist in her hair, pushing her down.

"Mmph." The little surprised sound she made reverberated around his cock.

"Do that again."

She lifted her eyes in question, her mouth still full of his malehood.

"Make that sound again." He guided her head up and down over his cock as a shudder ran up his inner thighs. He wouldn't last ten more seconds at this rate. And he shouldn't waste his seed in her mouth—not when he needed her to conceive.

She hummed while her head bobbed up and down.

He thrust up to meet her, balls tight, his eyes rolling back in his head. In and out he pumped, wanting it to last forever, knowing he should stop before he came. "Enough," he barked.

She jerked off him, her hair mussed, a confusion on her face. Her pretty peach-tipped breasts shifted as she moved.

"Good girl." He forced some control, reached out and caressed her cheek with his thumb. "Lie down on your belly, legs spread wide."

He helped her into position because her bound wrists made it awkward to lower herself. After he climbed over her, he brushed her hair away from her shoulder and nipped her ear. "You are so *vecking* beautiful like that."

She moaned and lifted her ass in the air, offering her dripping pussy to him.

He fit his cock between her parted thighs and shoved in.

Another moan from his slave. Her arousal rate already flashed at ninety percent.

Yes, they were sexually compatible. More than he'd ever dreamed.

He rocked his pelvis, gliding in and out of her, savoring the tight fit and the perfect sight of her pinned beneath him, her wrists bound behind her back, her shimmering hair fanned out beside her.

"So *vecking* beautiful."

He shoved in deep and came, only remembering to reach around and diddle her clit at the last minute. It didn't matter—her muscles squeezed the moment he orgasmed, timed in perfect harmony to his rhythm.

She fit him.

~.~

Zander released her wrist cuffs and kissed the back of her neck before he got up and went to the washtube. A gooey warmth swam through her, not only from the orgasm, but from Zander's show of affection—the kiss, the muttered words about her beauty.

It made her want to be the best slave possible, to earn more of his approval. If it made her life here easier, was it so wrong to give him what he wanted? A submissive, obedient servant, willing to part her legs any time he demanded it?

Zander emerged, dressed in a finely woven white tunic and pants, with a rainbow-hued mantle over his shoulders.

She leaned up on her elbows and opened her mouth to ask him where he was going, but then closed it again. He would find that too forward.

He hadn't missed it, though. His understanding of her personality seemed to improve daily. "You may speak."

A shiver of desire went through her at the words. Why did she like it when he treated her so far beneath him? Did it make her admire him more for his elevated power?

"I was wondering if you're going somewhere special today?"

"It is visiting day. You will not be permitted from my chamber today because the pod will be full of outsiders."

She remembered Gunt's explanation. This was the day Zandians could recharge with the crystal light or visit with Prince Zander. When he left her alone in the room, he locked her in the cage. Her stomach tightened.

"Must I stay in the cage?"

"You must. Go and wash up if you wish first. If you're a good girl and you go in without protest, I will let you attend the weekly meal with me tonight."

The promise of any variety to break up her day had her scrambling to be his "good girl." She jumped into the washtube, dressed, and went into the cage without protest.

"I'll have your first two meals sent in and the servants will let you out to stretch." He turned the cage so his face was inches from hers through the bars. He touched her nose. "You please me."

Three simple words—they filled her with such joy. *Veck,* she was totally losing it. Wasn't there an ancient Earth term for this? Oh yes, Stockholm syndrome. She supposed it was a natural human instinct to bond with the person responsible for her survival. But what would her father think? He must be rolling over in his grave right now.

She noticed Zander's multi-colored mantle shimmered with thousands of tiny crystals woven into the fabric. A gasp left her lips and she propped herself up on one elbow to see better.

Zander fingered the mantle with an apologetic, almost embarrassed expression. "What? The crystals? They are from Zandia." He lifted the edge and fed it through the cage bars for her to examine. "This was my father's. Personally, I'd like to forego the throne and royalty thing—skip the adjudication, but my advisors believe it brings our species hope. The elders weep and reach out to touch it. I'm like a relic of what's been lost."

She caught her breath, stunned at how much of the real Zander she'd just glimpsed. "It's beautiful."

"I think...when my species see the crystals and the colors, it affirms who they remember themselves to be."

When she brushed the pad of her index finger across a crystal, a wave of power rolled over her. If she had not been lying down, it might have knocked her off her feet. It felt like traveling at time warp speed. Her teeth buzzed and thousands of images fell into her head at once.

Although the sensations were not unpleasant, she jerked her finger away from the soft fabric and glowing crystals.

"What do you feel when you touch them?" she asked, forcing her voice to sound steady.

He frowned and she realized she'd done it again—her reaction had been paranormal, out of range. "I did not choose to rule over any other being. It was a position forced upon me when the Finn killed off the rest of my species."

"Of course," she said quickly to soothe his defensiveness. She hadn't meant to touch a nerve.

He plucked a crystal from the mantle, tearing the threads. Reaching through the bars of her cage, he pressed it to her forehead, between her brows.

A shock of energy range through her like an electric charge.

"Zandian females decorated themselves in crystals. They pierced their nipples and navels, their faces and anywhere else they wanted decoration."

Her entire body trembled—both from the crystal he'd stuck to her forehead and the idea of wearing more. Something about it excited her on a cellular level, thrills spiraling out in waves from all the places he'd suggested.

Something buzzed on his cuff, and he drew back from the cage. "Be good, little slave. I'll come for you later."

The heat burned into her forehead and traveled down her body to her pulsing pussy, which had grown moist just at his admonishment to be good.

It took effort to make herself speak, but she managed to croak. "Yes, master."

The moment the door slid shut behind him, the images rushed in again. Far too many to follow—too fast. Her vision blurred and nausea forced her to shove herself more upright—as much as she could in the small space.

A fierce Zandian warrior flashed before her eyes. He was older than Zander—perhaps by ten solar cycles. Flanking him, she saw armies of ships and warriors of a variety of species.

With a flick of her fingers, she removed the crystal from her forehead and drew a measured breath to slow her heart rate.

She didn't know what all this meant, but it was far too dangerous, no matter how sweet the energy of the crystal felt. The last thing she needed was to get confused about what she should and should not know about.

~.~

Zander found himself oddly excited about the prospect of bringing Lamira to the weekly meal. It was probably a terrible idea. She wasn't trained well enough yet. She still tested him, still sassed. But she had improved over the past several days.

But if he was honest, he'd admit wanting her near him wasn't a rational decision. She'd become an addiction. When he spent the day away from her, he felt itchy. On edge. He burned to have her writhing naked under his hands, to hear the little cries she made when he took her, to examine every inch of her glorious body.

The *vecking* human was becoming a huge distraction. And, like any addiction, he couldn't pull himself back.

His guard Gunt pressed his palm to the screen outside his door, so it was open when he arrived. He nodded at the male as he passed him, his eyes already on the cage.

"Have you been a good slave, Lamira?"

She shook the bars of her cage impatiently but wisely held her tongue. She was learning.

He opened the door and caught her waist as she launched herself out.

"Washroom," she murmured, twisting out of his grasp.

He let her go, watching her ass sway as she scampered to the washroom.

When she re-emerged, she held up the dress he'd sent a servant to buy today for her to wear. A simple Zandian traditional dress, it was constructed of white linen with a halter-style neckline and long, slim skirt. "Is this for me to wear?" Color had risen to her cheeks.

Was she excited?

"Yes. Try it on to see if it fits."

She started to go back into the washroom then blushed, as if realizing she had nothing to hide from him, and stripped out of what he called her "cage clothes"—clothing he permitted her to wear in the cage on days he had to have servants sent in to care for her. The dress slithered over her head and down her lovely curves, fitting perfectly. Her skin looked pale compared to a Zandian's, but she looked no less beautiful than any Zandian female he'd seen—live or in a hologram.

She must have seen the appreciation in his eyes because she blushed and dropped her eyes. "Does it look nice?" She spread her fingers at her sides, as if presenting herself.

He held his hand out. "Almost perfect. Come here."

She crossed the room and stood before him.

"Release wrist cuffs. Release ankle cuffs. Release collar." The soft leather pieces dropped to the floor. He wound a bit of the ceremonial rainbow fabric around her neck. "This will show you're mine, without screaming slave." He cupped her chin and lifted her face. "Now, listen to me. You will not speak unless spoken to. Keep your eyes lowered and speak respectfully. Any transgressions and I will bare your ass and lay you over my lap for punishment in front of every being at my table. Understand?"

Her lower jaw thrust forward at a defiant angle. She didn't like that.

"Or do we need to get that spanking out of the way before we go?"

He saw the flash of arousal projected from his cuff at the same time he picked up her physical cues.

She shook her head. "No, master."

"Hold your skirt up."

She blinked, her breath quickening. Her fingertips dragged up the hem of her skirt until it rose above her waist. "Like this?"

He sauntered around behind her and hooked his thumbs in the waistband of her panties, dragging them down to her ankles. "Step out."

She obeyed.

"Spread your legs wide."

She widened her stance.

"Don't move." He spanked her buttocks with the flat of his hand, first the right side, then the left.

To his delight, Lamira stayed perfectly still, not trying to get away or dodge the blows. Her little gasps made music with the sound of his palm striking her flesh.

After a dozen slaps, he ignored the projected readout, showing she was eighty-five percent aroused, and swiped two fingers between her legs to test for himself. "Lamira, you're soaking wet."

He wanted to make her bend over and grab her ankles so he could *veck* her raw right there, but a wicked idea occurred to him. "Don't move," he ordered again, and gave her ass a slap as he walked to the box of implements and retrieved two bullet vibrators. When he returned to stand behind her, he gripped her hips and tilted her pelvis so her ass lifted and her back arched. "Show me what's mine," he said, his voice thick.

She hollowed her back, arching even more.

He rubbed the first bullet in her moisture and slid it inside her, *vecking* her with it until she whimpered with need. With her lubricant providing ample coating, he switched it to her anus, pushing it against her little rosette.

She jerked and tucked her tail like a *sharkhound*, pulling her cheeks together and forward.

He slapped each cheek. "Bad girl. Open up or you'll get a punishment spanking with the wooden paddle."

She whimpered, but her arousal rate had reached almost 100 percent.

"Are you scared?" he murmured, his lips close to her ear. With his left hand cradling her throat, he used the right to push the tip of the bullet vibrator against her sphincter muscles. "Or merely ashamed to have me touch you in a place so personal?"

Her chest rose and fell, the fine fabric of the dress shifting over her breasts with the movement. She moistened her lips with the tip of her tongue. "A little of both."

"I'm not going to hurt you. I'm just torturing you because I know you like it, no matter how much you lie." He eased the plug into her ass and pumped it a few times before pushing it all the way in. After delivering another sharp slap to her pink backside, he plunged the second vibrator into her pussy and turned them both on.

Lamira whirled to face him, shock streaking her face. She fell against his chest, her little hands fisting in the fabric of his tunic. Her eyes pleaded, desperation simmering just below the surface. "Zander!"

He deactivated both vibrators. "Who do you belong to?"

"You, my lord." Her legs wobbled, so he took her elbow and guided her toward the door.

"Good. Remember the rules and I won't have to punish you publicly."

He saw a retort in her expression, but she clamped her lips closed, too smart to test him.

~.~

She stopped as he opened the door. She'd never put her panties back on.

Gunt stood at his post, his cold stare boring a hole in her head. He didn't like seeing her happy with Zander—or so it seemed.

She tugged Zander's arm, trying to get him to come back into the chamber.

He turned, lips thinning.

"My...um..." She jerked her head toward the panties on the floor.

Zander followed her gaze and his lips turned up in a sexy smirk. "Leave them. Let's go."

Oh Mother Earth, what a trial. Her pussy practically gushed with moisture from all the attention he'd just given her. Her entire body must be at least fifty degrees hotter than usual. After the disquieting visions produced by the crystal that morning, Zander had brought her firmly back into her body.

She walked on shaky legs beside Zander, who kept one hand around her back. It was an oddly tender gesture, which only served to further discombobulate her.

Zander led her to the Great Hall, which had been transformed with a long table that took up the entire length of the hall, beautifully dressed in colorful fabrics and crystal centerpieces.

She drew in a breath at the magnificence of it.

Zander glanced at her and smiled.

The table was crowded with Zandians, who all stood when they entered, facing them like they were royalty. Which, of course, one of them was.

Zander inclined his head, and his fellow Zandians bowed back. He drew back a chair next to the head of the table and indicated it was for her. Once she sat, he took the place at the head. She realized that everyone was gazing, not at their prince, but at her. Well, yes, she was the only human present.

"Drop your eyes," Zander said in an undertone.

Of course, her immediate reaction to his order was to swivel a defiant gaze on him.

He raised a brow and activated both vibrators inside her.

She caught the edge of the table, eyes glued on her plate in an effort to control her reaction. Heat washed over her skin; her pussy leaked moisture onto the skirt of her dress. Knuckles turning white, she ground her molars, trying to block out the intense sensations. She wanted to crawl under the table to hump her hand until she climaxed by the time Zander turned it off.

"Lamira, this is Lium, my tactical engineer. He's responsible for purchasing and handling our airships."

She looked across the table at the grizzled Zandian the prince indicated. His face was lined and short hair had turned white, but he looked every inch a warrior, with massive shoulders and a thick neck.

Lium looked at her but didn't acknowledge the introduction, so she followed his lead and said nothing.

"Beside him is Erick, my trade and business advisor."

Erick did not appear as old as Lium, but, still, like everyone in the pod but her, had to be at least twice Zander's age. He actually smiled at her and inclined his head. "How do you find your new life?"

She glanced at Zander as a thousand answers clogged in her throat. The question shouldn't come as such a surprise. How did she answer such a question? *Other than being kept in a cage and tortured with two vibrating devices at once, fine.* Or how about, *I love it when your hot Zandian prince spanks my bare ass and shoves his huge purple cock into me, but I'm not so crazy about subservience.* Because he seemed kind and genuinely friendly, she gave the most gracious reply her mind conjured. "It's beautiful here."

Zander seemed to doubt her reply, because his eyes narrowed.

Fearing he would turn on the vibrating devices again, she adopted a pleading expression.

One corner of his lips lifted.

"You already know Daneth. Next to him is Seke, my master at arms."

Another massive warrior, this one a bit younger than Lium, but still much older than Zander. Scars decorated his middle-aged face. She saw pain etched into the lines there, too. A flash of claircognizance told her he'd lost his wife and infant in the massacre. The weight of his tragedy punched her in the chest. She realized everyone at this table bore similar losses. They may live in a beautiful pod, but they had suffered—perhaps no less than she and her mother had suffered.

Now she understood the importance of Zander breeding. If the prince was the youngest of his species, he'd be the only chance for it to survive. It also explained why he'd chosen a human—clearly there were no females of breeding age. Only three females sat at the table, and they were all ancient.

He introduced her to the other half-dozen Zandians who sat near them. From what she gathered, the table was organized by status, with the prince and his most powerful advisors beside him and the lowest servants who weren't responsible for bringing the food at the far end.

Zander's hand idly tangled in her hair as he listened to a report from Erick on a business deal.

Barr himself arrived to serve Zander's food, and his face broke into a broad smile when he saw her seated beside the prince. "Good evening, my lord," he said with a bow as he set a steaming bowl of soup in front of Zander. "Good evening, Lamira."

She straightened and beamed back at the old chef. "Good evening, Barr. That smells delicious."

Servants arrived and placed matching bowls in front of the rest of the diners, including her. "I didn't know you were eating here, or I would have served you a smaller portion. Save room for the rest of the meal, little human." Barr liked to tease her about how small her stomach was.

Zander glared at the chef, whose skin colored darker purple as he bowed and backed hastily away. Every being took a sudden interest in their soup, so she did the same. Was her prince actually jealous? Or had she shamed him in some way? She hoped not.

After that, she did keep her eyes lowered, though she listened in on the conversations with interest. Despite the dwindling numbers of the species, the Zandians must be excellent in business, with trade in a variety of sectors. That must be how the pod came to be so opulently decorated and how Zander planned to launch a campaign against the vast population of the Finn.

After the soup came huge platters of ostrich meat, wild bluegrain, and Relo sea vegetables. She realized now why Barr thought she ate so little. The Zandians piled their plates high and emptied them several times while she only finished a half a plate of the rich, exquisitely-prepared dishes. Barr served a blueberry wine that made her head swim. It loosened the Zandians tongues, and soon they were all talking in louder voices, laughing and gesturing like old friends.

A pang of remorse for something she'd never known stabbed her heart—this sense of family, of community they all shared. She wanted to belong with them, wanted to be a part of it all.

When she had finished eating and Zander filled his third plate, he tugged her onto his lap, holding her on one knee while he ate and talked. He stroked his hand up her inner thigh.

She jerked and held her breath, her arousal so close to the edge as it was.

He shoved her knees apart, angling his fingers straight over her clit.

She bit her lips, closing her mouth on a cry.

Zander hadn't looked at her once, intent on some conversation with Erick about the price of sand rocks. That didn't stop him from turning on the vibrator in her pussy.

"No," she whispered. Her thighs pressed closed around his fingers. "Please, Zander."

The vibrator in her anus zoomed to life.

Please, no. Mother Earth, no.

"Please," she whimpered in his ear. "Please, I'll be good. I'll be a good slave."

Zander still didn't take his eyes from Erick, but his lips curved into a smug smile. He slapped her thighs open and smacked her pussy twice.

She bit her lip so hard she drew blood. Zander's sense of smell must be better than a human's because he sniffed and turned, his brows drawn together with concern.

He frowned and cupped her chin, taking her lip into his mouth and sucking.

She came.

Yes, right there, sitting on his lap in front of his entire household, she climaxed.

Zander laughed and turned the vibrators off. "Go back to my chamber little human. Take off your clothes and wait for me on the sleepdisk. I'll be in soon." He murmured the words, but she feared everyone at the great, long table knew exactly what had happened and what was going on. Her cheeks burned with embarrassment.

She stood on trembling legs and affected a sort of curtsy.

Sweet Mother Earth, what was happening to her? This alien had a terrifying effect on her. She needed to get a grip. Fast.

Chapter Six

Three days later, Zander fingered the laser gun hidden beneath his robe. He had four other weapons also hidden within quick reach. Seke and Lium flanked him as they faced Joan-Angeline, the Ocretion smuggler.

"Your ships are on the way. I require the remaining payment now."

He shook his head. "Payment will come when I have the ships in my possession, as we agreed on."

She smiled an ugly smile. Half her teeth were blackened or missing. "I'm changing the arrangement."

He turned, daring to give her his back. Seke and Lium would cover him, and the feigned nonchalance was more important than his personal safety now. "Deal's off." He walked away, not turning to look back as he spoke.

"Wait a moment, Zander the Zandian."

He didn't stop.

"The ships are here," she called out.

He paused, but didn't turn.

She gave a deep laugh. "In the hangar. Come, I'll show you."

He pivoted slowly and folded his arms across his chest. "Stop playing games with me, Joan-Angeline."

Again, the toothy smile. "No games. I have your ships. Let's go. You'll be satisfied, I assure you."

He snorted. He didn't believe her assurances for a millisecond, but if she had the fighting ships he'd been seeking, she'd be the first of many who promised to actually deliver. And he needed these ships. Without them, the liberation of Zandia would be impossible.

He, Seke, and Lium followed her down a metal walkway to a large hangar. There, nine beat-up fighting ships stood parked.

"I paid you for a dozen."

"You paid *half* the cost of a dozen. And I require the remaining half now. They were difficult to acquire. The price has gone up."

Once more, he called her bluff. "No deal. These ships may not even be airworthy. I'll take them for the money I already paid, no more."

"Ah, sorry, Prince Zander, but I have another buyer. If you don't take them, he will."

Zander hesitated. This might be true. He'd been attempting to acquire an air fleet for the past sixteen lunar cycles and these were the first he'd seen. He couldn't be the only being the galaxy who wanted to buy ships on the black market. Joan-Angeline had maybe fifteen beings standing around with guns. None of them looked particularly smart. The three Zandians could probably take them all in a fight. They were all well-trained warriors. But he had honor. He wouldn't steal what he had pledged to buy, even if Joan-Angeline didn't deserve it. "The ships are mine. I financed their purchase. Because Zandians have honor, I will pay the price we agreed upon, but only for the ships that are here."

Joan-Evangeline puffed her fat cheeks and stared at him, her bug eyes never blinking.

He kept his knees soft, his hand on his weapon, ready if she struck.

"Load the ships into their carrier," she snapped at her underlings, whirling and walking away.

Lium and Seke didn't relax, still as alert as he to any danger.

The smugglers loaded the fighting ships onto his carrier, though, while Joan-Evangeline stood guard at the door to make sure he didn't leave without paying. He counted out the steins and placed them in a burlap sack, which he tossed to her when the transfer of the ships was complete. She gave him another toothy grin. "Nice doing business with you Zander of Zandia."

He inclined his head. Zandians didn't lie, and he'd be lying if he said the same about her. They boarded the craft carrier, and he took the controls to fly them out of Joan-Evangeline's docking station and back to his pod. Only when they had flown several miles without a tail did he begin to relax.

He finally had fighter ships. Now all he needed was an army.

Chapter Seven

Lamira touched the first sprout of a watermelon plant from her row of starts. Her pussy was raw and sore from fresh use and her limbs wobbled like they were made of rubber. It must be the recent orgasm that made her spirits soar now. She shouldn't be this excited over new plant starts.

After she'd made her list of supplies, Zander had found a catalog and let her leaf through the holograms and pick everything herself. He'd allowed her to buy several types of exorbitantly expensive heirloom seeds, originally grown on Earth, before the planet was destroyed by the overpopulation of the Ocretions. He'd paid for the best soil and beautiful pots, since the "garden" would actually be in his great hall. He'd even ordered two of his servants to assist her. She'd planted the seeds four days ago, and already some had sprouted.

Life as Zander's breeder continued to befuddle her. The confinement and degradation maddened her. The sex, though, while rough and hard, brought her to heights she'd never known existed. She liked it too much.

She checked the timer Zander had given her. He allowed her to leave his chamber on limited excursions without guard for set periods of time. If she didn't return by her curfew, he would punish her. She hadn't dared disobey. She'd pushed hard for the freedom, and fought especially not to have a guard accompany her, not wanting to be alone again with the thief Gunt.

Three minutes until Zander expected her back in his chambers. *Veck.* She'd lost track of time. She ran down the lemon-hued corridor, dusting her hands on her skirt as she went. She arrived at the door and lifted her chin, waiting for Gunt to let her in. She hated the few moments when she had to pass him at his post.

He didn't move, but his horns twitched. "Have you reconsidered my offer?"

Seriously? The dungheap wouldn't give up. "I wouldn't *veck* you if you were the last male in the galaxy," she hissed, reaching past him to open the door herself. Of course, it didn't work. It required the handprint of someone with authorization to open the door, and apparently hers didn't fit that requirement.

His eyes and skin a dark-purple, he shoved her up against the door and curled his fingers punitively, painfully into her clothed sex. "You'll regret that, you *vecking* slave-whore."

She shoved hard against him, but he didn't budge. His fingers groped with bruising intensity.

The door slid open and Gunt sprang away from her. She whirled and practically fell into Zander's arms.

He ignored his guard and dragged an appreciative gaze over her. His hunger showed in the darkening of his horns, the way they tilted toward her. Her body reacted to his nearness, allowing her to put aside Gunt's nasty pawing. Soon, she would tell Zander about it, when she knew him a little better and was sure he would believe her.

"Ah. I thought I might have to punish you."

Her pussy clenched. Zander looked incredible in a body-hugging exercise suit, his huge muscles bulging. It took great resistance not to reach out and touch his hard chest. "No, my lord."

"Come." He pushed her into the room.

She balked. He would put her in the cage. That's what he did when he left her in his room. He didn't trust her alone in there. Probably didn't trust her with his communication devices. "Are you going to exercise, my lord?"

He gripped her upper arm and pulled her toward the cage. "Yes."

She tried to slow their steps with no result. "May I watch you? I'll be good. I'll kneel in the corner and won't make a sound."

He raised an eyebrow, as if suspicious it was a trick.

Well, maybe it was. But the only trick was getting out of the boredom and claustrophobia of the damn cage.

"Please?" She gave him her best pleading slave eyes, which she knew he loved.

His horns stiffened and twitched in her direction. "Promise you'll be good?"

She nodded quickly. "I promise. I won't disturb you a bit."

He tugged her elbow in that commanding way he had. "Let's go."

"Really?" She scurried along beside him. "Thank you."

"Don't make me regret it." He could be gruff, but she'd found he wasn't terrible. Over the past week, he'd only punished her three more times, each time for disrespect. Despite all the new implements Daneth had brought him, he'd only used his hand and each spanking had concluded with a rough breeding session, which she had come to love.

He bred with her once or twice a day. He didn't always hold her afterward the way he had her second day, but when he did, she melted—turning as slave-y and submissive as a human who'd been born and bred to serve a man. And she hated herself for it.

Gunt's eyes burned a hole in her back as they walked away, as always. She'd decided he was harmless. If he really thought he could get away with raping her, he would've already accomplished it. Still, she planned to avoid him at all costs.

Zander led her to a room she had not seen before. Like the dining hall, it was lit with natural sunlight magnified by a giant crystal. The room was small with a domed ceiling and raised platform. Seke, the fierce-looking master at arms stood on the platform holding a wooden staff as tall as his body.

Zander pointed silently to a wall and left her, walking up to face the older male and offering a soundless bow.

She knelt with her back to the wall and marveled at Zander's behavior. It was the first time he'd shown subservience to another. In a moment, she saw why. Seke's staff shot out, directly in line with Zander's head. He ducked and swung a foot out to knock the middle-aged male off balance, but Seke jumped, looking as spry as a child.

He swung the staff at Zander once again. Zander dived away into a graceful forward roll.

She bit her lips against the gasp that rose at his magnificence.

The two continued sparring wordlessly, shocking her with their athleticism and the pure art behind the fighting. Clearly, Zander had studied combat arts for most of his life. Watching him fight made her blood heat with desire. Her taut nipples scraped the fabric of the dress she wore, and her pussy soaked her panties with arousal.

She shifted her buttocks over one heel, hoping to press her sex against it to alleviate the growing pressure there. It didn't work.

Zander's gaze flicked to her.

His teacher nearly took Zander's head off with a sword—they'd picked up new weapons several rounds before—but Zander dropped to the ground and rolled out of the way, springing back to his feet and going on the offensive.

Their tussle grew more aggressive, and Zander's fierce determination coupled with the sheer physicality and feline grace of his moves had her clit pulsing, her skin on fire, her breath uneven.

At last, they finished. They both bowed, and Zander spoke to him in their own tongue. The older male's thoughtful gaze flicked to her, but he left the chamber without another word. The moment the door snicked shut, Zander strode over to her and hauled her to her feet. He shoved her against the wall and gripped her jaw, bringing his gorgeous face close to hers. "Bad slave."

She sucked in her breath. What had she done?

"How was I supposed to concentrate when your readouts were flashing your arousal levels the whole time?"

She flushed, her fear at his sudden assault instantly morphing to wanton need.

His thumb slid between her lips and she sucked on it. He attacked her with his mouth, kissing her. It was like no kiss she'd seen or experienced before. His tongue disciplined her, lashing between her lips. His teeth sank into her lower lip before he sucked it into his mouth. He held her head immobile for the onslaught, not allowing her to control any of it.

He pulled back, his eyes a glittering dark-violet. "You're trembling. Are you scared?"

She couldn't make her lips move to speak, but she shook her head no.

"Am I hurting you?"

She licked her lips. "Desire," she managed to rasp out, her voice sounding hoarse.

He seized her again, cupping her ass and lifting her from the floor. "Do you want me to wash first?"

Was he really asking *her*? His slave? If she said yes, would he stop this and clean himself for her?

It didn't matter. She wasn't going to find out, because she needed him desperately, and his masculine sweat only heightened her lust.

"I like you this way," she purred and wrapped her legs around his waist, clutching at his shoulders.

He released his cock from his pants and yanked her panties to the side.

"I'm going to *veck* you right here, little slave. Right here in the exercise room." He speared her, his huge cock filling her and taking her breath away.

With her body pinned to the wall, he slammed in and out of her, asserting his claim over her with each aggressive stroke.

Take me.

She wanted it—needed release more than anything.

"I should take your ass to punish you for distracting me," he said, pounding so hard she thought he might crush her against the wall. Though he continued to threaten anal sex, he had yet to follow through.

"No, no, no," she moaned.

"You were a bad girl."

"No," she protested.

"No? Then you'd better squeeze my cock as hard as you can, little slave...*ungh*," Zander groaned when she obeyed.

He neared climax. She recognized the way his face twitched, his eyes almost black-violet.

"*Now*, little slave. You'd better get ready. Climax, or I take your ass." He orgasmed, thrusting deep inside her and holding her, pinned to the wall by his cock alone.

She screamed, her muscles convulsing around his cock in spasmodic squeezing, milking it for his seed. She'd been ready to come since the moment he began fighting, so the intensity of the orgasm made lights dance before her eyes.

When it passed, she went boneless, a limp rag, hardly able to hold her own head up.

A couple of tears leaked from the outer corners of her eyes.

Zander licked them and closed his eyes as if relishing the taste of her tears. "Did I hurt you?" His voice had gone tender, now. Holy star, how she loved this side of him.

She shook her head, even though he'd surely left bruises all up and down her back. She didn't care. It had been explosively satisfying.

He scooped her into his arms, yanked her dress down, and carried her back to his chamber.

When they passed Gunt at the door, he narrowed his eyes at her, his mouth contorting as if he'd just eaten an insect. She didn't think Zander noticed, but was grateful when the door snicked closed behind them.

Zander arranged her in her cage with a pillow under her hips to keep his seed in. She didn't even mind the cage—her body still glowed from the sex, her pussy pulsing and sore, her blood humming.

He set a timer. "When that goes off, you may move. Take off your clothes and wait for my return. I have a few things to do after I go in the washtube."

Her eyelids grew heavy and she drifted off to sleep, remembering the feel of Zander's large hands on her body.

~.~

"My lord, a word?" Gunt, the guard stationed outside Zander's room stopped him before he went in.

His mind on all the things he was going to do with his naked slave, he stopped with a touch of impatience. "Yes?"

"Your slave, my lord. She's been trying to escape."

He stared, his mind stuttering on Gunt's words. "She can't escape." Every exit in the pod was guarded, and every guard in the pod understood she was not to be allowed out. Even if she found an exit—and he hadn't heard that she had gone anywhere but where she was supposed to go—she would never be permitted through it.

"She offered her body to me in exchange for helping her escape, my lord."

Zander's torso flushed with a flash of cold, followed closely by red-hot rage. He lunged at Gunt, wrapping his fist in the guard's tunic and shoving his back against the wall. "She *what*?"

The guard's eyes widened in shock. "I didn't do it—I wouldn't, my lord," he stammered. "I told her no, of course."

He wanted to skin her alive. Lamira—*his* little slave, *his* breeder—had offered her *vecking* affections to his guards.

He dropped the male and activated the door, striding into his room, ready for battle.

"Cage open." He stormed to it and grasped her ankle, yanking her roughly out.

"Zander," she screamed in alarm.

"Do not speak my name." His voice sounded like cold steel. It sounded more steady than he felt. He dropped her in a cowering heap at his feet.

Veck. Veckity veck veck. Not Lamira. Not *his vecking* slave.

"What's wrong?" She stood up and tilted her deceitful face up to him.

"What's wrong?" he repeated. "I have learned about your attempted escape."

She went still, proving the truth of his words. *Veck.* He'd still somehow hoped it wasn't true.

"I beg your pardon?" Her voice sounded choked.

"Oh yes, you'll be begging my pardon for a long time to come," he raged. The level of his anger was beyond any he'd ever experienced. How could a little human female inspire such depth of emotion in him?

He grasped her wrists and hauled her to the center of the room. With her arms pulled up over her head, he attached her cuffs to a strap hung from the ceiling. He pulled it taut until it lifted her up onto her toes.

"Zander, Zander, please." She twisted and danced from the bindings, her naked body mocking him with its perfection. "Tell me what's going on. What do you mean, my attempted escape?"

He strode to the box of implements and picked up a thick leather strap, sliced at the end to form two tongues. "Why don't you tell me?" Pure ice in his voice. Ice he didn't feel. In fact, he'd never boiled so hot in his life. *Veck*, he'd never felt this much emotion ever—not even when his parents were killed and his planet overtaken.

This was what came of breeding a human. Her overly large emotions had somehow affected his own.

He raised his arm and took aim, applying the strap across the center of her buttocks.

She screamed and twisted away from him, dancing on her toes. A red stripe bloomed across her flesh.

He shook his head. "Hold your position, Lamira, or this strap will fall on your hips and legs and hurt far worse."

Her full lips trembled and green eyes swam with tears.

No. She would not gain his sympathy. Not this time.

He snapped the strap across her quivering cheeks again.

She cried out and danced away, but this time returned to position.

"Tell me about your plan to escape."

"I have none!" she cried out.

If he didn't know humans always lied, he'd think he heard genuine indignation in her voice.

"Liar," he thundered, whipping her even harder.

Her scream hurt his ears, but he gritted his teeth and delivered another stroke and then another. The strap left a crisscrossing of puffy red welts across her buttocks.

"I don't know what you're talking about." She was crying already. He smelled the salt of her tears but had no desire to lick them this time.

"You betrayed me."

Betray was a strong word. She wasn't his mate, she was a slave. And slaves by nature try to escape. It was the reason he kept her in a cage, after all. But he had no rational outlook on what she had done. It burned in his gut, made him want to put his fist through a wall and smash everything in his chamber. Offering herself to Gunt. *Gunt.*

He whipped her again, across the backs of her legs this time.

The terror in her scream did move him, though he wished it did not. He wouldn't whip her there anymore.

Instead, he whipped her ass, three times in rapid succession.

She danced and screamed and wept.

"Gunt told me."

"Told you what?" she screeched. "That he's stealing crystals from you and selling them on the black market?"

"Stop your lies," he yelled, whipping her again. "He told me how you offered him sex if he'd help you escape. You deceitful little whore!"

"He's lying!" she screamed back at him. "He offered that to *me*, not the other way around."

"Zandians don't lie, only humans have such little honor," he shouted and whipped her three, four, five more times.

He stopped, struggling to slow his breath and regain his temper. It was all her fault.

Her ass was a swollen mess—covered in angry red welts. He couldn't go on—not without breaking her delicate skin. He unhooked her wrists and tossed her on his sleeping platform.

She curled up in a little ball, hiccupping.

Unbelievably, his cuff flashed her readout.

Forty percent aroused.

She'd been aroused by the whipping?

Well, he'd breed her then. He didn't care if he hurt her doing it. Hell, he should take her ass for this, but he didn't have the control to be careful enough not to cause her real damage.

His head still swam with the shock of her deceit, her betrayal. He'd wanted to pound Gunt's face in when he told him she'd offered herself up to him.

He grabbed her thighs and yanked her to the edge of the sleepdisk on her stomach.

She turned her tear-streaked face to the side, but stared only at the wall. She was listening, perhaps, for what he would do next.

He nudged her feet apart and she spread her legs, fully compliant, despite her pitiful sobs.

Something in his chest constricted.

No. He wouldn't feel sorry for her. She deserved her punishment.

He shoved his pants down enough to free his cock.

She offered no resistance when he rubbed the head of his cock over her entrance. In fact, he found her pussy slick and welcoming.

He pushed in. His nostrils flared at the glory of her tight, moist heat. Even now, even after what she'd done, he wanted her as much as always.

Damn Daneth and his *vecking* program, picking this *vecking* human for him to breed with.

He slammed inside her, slapping his loins against her flayed ass without care.

She whimpered, still crying softly into his blankets.

No. No pity for her.

He pumped his hips, ignoring her readouts flashing her arousal rate. He didn't care about her orgasm this time. He would leave his seed and she would take it up, like a good slave or she'd never leave her *vecking* cage again.

With punishing strokes, he pounded into her, squeezing his eyes closed to block out the noise in his head and the tightness in his chest. He didn't draw it out on purpose. It certainly wasn't her weeping that delayed his orgasm, but he *vecked* her so long, he grew tired of the position.

He flipped her over.

Her wide, frightened eyes made him grit his teeth. He would not be soft on her.

He clipped her wrists and ankles to the posts on his sleepdisk, spreading her limbs wide.

Her belly fluttered with her sobbing breaths, chest heaved. "I didn't do it, Zander." Her reddened eyelids fluttered.

"Silence," he bellowed and slapped her face. It wasn't a hard slap. He would never mark her beautiful face. He covered her mouth with his hand and mounted her.

~.~

Lamira closed her eyes. She couldn't bear Zander's angry countenance. The only thing keeping her from utter desperation was the tiny voice in her head saying, *this means he cares*. Because surely he would not be so angry over his belief she'd offered herself to Gunt if he didn't feel something for her.

And that knowledge was as satisfying as his angry thrusts deep inside her. She needed this breeding—even as angry as he was. Even as helpless and vulnerable and hurting as she was. Her swollen ass flamed, tender and so raw against his soft sheets.

Zander growled and slammed into her three more times then came.

Her own body responded without any prompting, squeezing his cock, finding her finish in perfect synchronization to his. It was as if, despite all her mental rebellion, her body knew its master. It responded always to his presence, to his touch—whether harsh or gentle.

When he pulled out, he clipped her ankles to a hook on the ceiling, lifting her pelvis in the air with her striped ass on display.

She would have cried again, but she'd used up all her tears. She hung in her ridiculous position as numbness set in, a hollow right in the middle of her chest. She drew in a hiccupping breath and watched Zander turn away from her in disgust and stalk to the washroom once again.

He ignored her when he emerged, freshly washed. Walking to his work platform, he began flicking up holograms.

A light tap sounded at the door and it slid open.

"What?" Zander barked.

"Forgive me, my lord, but Lamira's monitors show signs of stress."

She couldn't see Daneth from her shameful position, but she had no doubt he had full view of her most intimate parts.

"I don't doubt it." Zander's voice was tight.

Daneth walked closer. She turned her face and closed her eyes as if that would keep him from examining her in intimate detail. "What happened?" he asked mildly.

"She offered herself to my guards in exchange for their help in escaping."

"That is not true," she gritted through clenched teeth.

"*Do not speak, slave,*" Zander thundered.

Daneth released her cuffs from their binds.

She rolled into a ball on her side, her legs and arms pricking with pins and needles as the blood returned to them.

"What happened to her back?"

Zander didn't answer for a moment, and then his voice sounded close to the sleepdisk, as if he'd come to inspect her with Daneth. "I bred her up against a wall," he said dully. "She told me I didn't hurt her. Yet another lie." The disgust in his voice made her chest ache.

"I will take her to the lab for monitoring, my lord."

"No." Zander's voice was hard. "She stays here, with me."

Daneth's footsteps moved away then returned. He put the fluid tube to her lips. "Drink."

She did because she was thirsty.

"Has she fed?"

"Not in hours, no."

"I'll send some food in. I recommend you allow her to rest. Stress will adversely impact her ability to breed."

"Yes, well, so will escaping," Zander snapped.

Daneth hesitated. "Of course, my lord." He left and she heard Zander return to his work platform.

Several minutes later a soft tap sounded at the door again. She flicked the blanket across her body to cover her nudity and curled back into a ball.

"Shall I put the food in the cage, my Lord?" a subservient voice asked.

She tensed, waiting for his answer. She really didn't want to go in the cage.

"Leave it over there by the sleeping platform."

A small kindness. She may want to hate him, but he wasn't all bad. She heard the clink of a tray being set on the floating table beside the sleeping platform. She ignored it.

"You may eat."

So imperious. A good slave would sit up and thank him for giving her food despite her punishment.

She wasn't a good slave. She wondered whether he would keep her. Yes his anger indicated he cared, but had he been pushed too far? The imagined loss of her position here, the thought of being sent back to the agrifarm came like a stab in the chest, even with her mother there. She didn't want to go.

Maybe she should beg. She should act more grateful, more slavey.

What would her life be here if she stayed? If she had his child?

She drifted to a semi-dream state, exhausted from the pain and angst, thinking about babies.

She *would* have his baby.

The knowledge came to her, as clear as the light through one of his crystals. *More than one child.*

It brought tears to her eyes. She rarely received information about her own life, and this particular piece of information felt precious, especially considering the ragged state of their relationship. She also hadn't expected the flood of joy she would experience over having a baby. She'd never thought about what it would feel like to bring a child into the world, had only been angry about the non-consensual plan to breed her.

She reached for more information about the child. Was it a boy? Or a girl?

Boy.

Would she raise it? Would she be its mother, or would Zander take the child from her? Would he be done with her once he had a child?

No.

She felt certain she would raise it. It was her baby. Her perfect halfling with green eyes and dark olive skin with a hint of purple. Beautiful in every way—a fat happy gurgling smiling cooing baby doing all the things that a perfect healthy baby should do. Her chest filled with so much love. It banished the grief of Zander's punishment and anger with her. She slipped into deeper sleep, peace settling around her like a blanket.

"My lord?"

She startled awake. Was someone else in the room?

No, Daneth's hologram hovered in mid-air. "Take a look at these data files."

"What's the subject?"

"Lium set up security recordings around the pod this solar cycle. I think you'll find these interesting."

Zander made a grumbling sound in his throat.

"These are the only two files of their kind. There is no other evidence of wrongdoing," Daneth said.

"This is my chamber."

She stilled. That was Gunt's voice.

"I should get back to Prince Zander."

And hers. She rolled over and opened her eyes, cringing to see the hologram of herself and Gunt standing in his chamber doorway. It unsettled her to see herself projected there, the fear and discomfort of the moment returning full force.

"I could help you around here. Protect you from the rest of them. Maybe even help you escape."
"Oh sure. And all I have to do is what? Suck your cock?"
"Not all. But yes. That's a start."
"No thanks."

Even knowing what was going to happen, it shocked her to watch Gunt's huge hand shoot out and grasp her throat.

Zander surged to his feet, his huge fist slamming down on his work screen.

"You think you're too good for me, vecking human?"

The hologram flickered off and a second one—the one of her and Gunt that morning—played.

"Repeat." Zander watched the tidbits one more time. When they ended, he stormed to the door, opened it, and slammed his fist into Gunt's ugly face.

She sat up, watching in fascinated horror as the prince followed Gunt to the ground, continuing to beat his face with his fists until two more guards arrived at a run.

"My lord, may we help you? What happened?"

He climbed off Gunt and snapped his head to crack his neck. "Take him to a dungeon cell," he growled.

They rushed in, seizing the unconscious guard's arms and dragging him off down the hall.

When he turned to her, Zander's purple skin looked paler than usual, his worried eyes searching her face. He came in, and the door slid shut behind him. His fingers curled into fists at his sides. He dropped them, though, and walked to the foot of the sleeping platform. "Lamira." His voice sounded strained. He crawled up over her.

She turned her face away. It burned hot with the intensity of the moment. She wanted to hide under the covers, her emotions too raw to meet Zander's eye after all that had passed between them.

"Lamira." He tugged her shoulder when she rolled away, then released her. "Lamira, I'm sorry."

The words sounded larger than the room. They filled the space, filled her.

"I made a...terrible mistake," he rasped. "Terrible." Out of the corner of her eye, she watched him rub his face. "I cannot undo it." This sounded to be as much to himself as to her. He sat beside her, leaning on one arm and gazing down. He stroked a lock of hair from her eyes.

She still refused to turn toward him, feeling too raw, too wronged. *Let him feel sorry.*

"I will grant you a boon to make amends. What can I give you?" He reached out to touch her again, this time resting his palm on her shoulder—lightly—as if afraid she'd shrug it off.

She drew a breath. The most wicked part of her wanted to make him suffer—to drag out his obvious distress and refuse to allow him to make amends. But the image of the baby flashed in her mind again. That image had changed her. Profoundly.

"Hold me."

"I beg your pardon?"

"The way you do sometimes after you breed with me."

He shook his head. "No, you don't understand. I will grant you a boon—make you a gift, or offer some freedom, as recompense for the suffering I caused you." He sounded stiff, formal. Like they were at an official proceeding or hearing.

"All I want is for you to hold me."

Was that moisture in Zander's eyes? He blinked rapidly and pulled back the covers to scoop her up into his arms. With his back against the wall, he settled, cradling her like a baby.

"Like this?" His raspy voice sounded pained.

She leaned her head on the hard, sculpted muscles of his shoulder and drank in his heat, his strength. This was the male who would be the father of her children. "Yes," she murmured.

He stroked up and down her arm in a non-demanding way, as he often did after breeding. "Why didn't you tell me—no, wait—I know you tried to tell me today, but why didn't you tell me when it happened?"

"I didn't want to cause any trouble. I'm trying to find my way here—to make friends. To learn to get along in my new home."

He stilled. "So you have accepted that you belong here? To me?"

Did she accept she was his slave and believe she belonged to him? No. She, like her father, believed humans should be free. But if she had to be someone's slave...she'd pick Zander to be her master over all others. "I am getting used to it," she said carefully.

He shifted her on his lap, and she winced at the pressure of her flayed skin brushing against his pants. He froze and lifted her into the air, scowling.

"Call Daneth," he snapped.

His cuff produced Daneth's head, floating right above her. She flinched.

"My lord."

"Bring something to ease her pain."

Daneth bowed his head. "Of course, my lord." The hologram disappeared.

"You should have told me. You are my slave—my female—and no other male should touch you, especially not from my own guard. I will kill—" He broke off and closed his eyes, as if reining in his temper. "I would have protected you. Did something else happen between you?" His violet gaze was intent.

"No, my lord."

"Is that truth?"

She nodded. "Truth."

He stroked her cheek. "If it had—if he had raped you, would you lie to me about it?"

She tensed. She might lie. She wouldn't want Zander to question the parentage of any child she conceived. "I told you, nothing happened. Remember how I begged you to let me go about the pod without a guard?"

Zander grimaced. "To avoid being with Gunt?"

She nodded. Her stomach rumbled.

Zander reached for the tray of food and picked up a piece of cheese. "You're hungry." He held it to her lips.

She closed her mouth and shook her head. "No, I'm not." She instantly regretted it.

Zander's eyes flashed and his body stiffened. "Even now you lie when I can clearly hear—"

"I meant, I'm too upset to eat."

"I don't understand."

She sighed and rolled her eyes. "My emotions affect my digestive organs. My stomach feels like it's tied in a knot. If I ate, it would make me sick."

Zander's expression grew sober and he drew her closer. "You're angry with me?"

"A little," she admitted.

"And what else? Your pain?" He ran his hand lightly over her swollen buttocks, and she hissed.

It was odd to have Zander always dissecting the things she said, never understanding normal human communication or emotions. It forced her into more self-awareness. And, for once, she wanted to confess the truth.

"You scared me."

Regret made Zander's handsome face droop. "I'm sorry, little human. Did you fear for your life? Your safety?"

She shrugged. "Maybe a little."

"I admit I was...upset." He used her word, as if trying it on for the first time. "But I would never cause you lasting harm. I wouldn't take it too far. I know humans are delicate. I knew when to stop."

She realized she believed him—perhaps she'd known it even at the time. Some little anxiety inside her settled.

A tap sounded at the door, and the screen on the back of it showed Daneth standing outside.

"Come in."

She squirmed, trying to extricate herself from Zander's arms, but he refused to let her go. He must have realized why she was uncomfortable, though, because he tugged a blanket up over her.

"Stress levels are still elevated," the doctor said, leaving out any greeting.

"What can you give her?"

Daneth produced a small gun.

"No." She tried once more to scramble out of Zander's grasp.

He caught her wrists in one of his hands and tugged them up, his other arm snugly around her waist. "Hush. This will make you feel better."

She twisted around, her legs thrashing underneath her. "No, it will make *you* feel better. I don't want to get—"

Zander held her immobile and the shot spiked in and out of her arm—a sharp prick.

"Ow!"

"It works on the central nervous system. It will calm her stress as well as alleviate pain. It should take effect in five minutes."

"I didn't ask you for that, you know—" she growled through clenched teeth, still thrashing against Zander's hold.

Zander ignored her, looking up at Daneth. "How did you know?"

The physician shrugged. "She appeared genuinely indignant—as though she'd been wronged."

~.~

Wronged. That was the understatement of the day. Guilt tightened his chest and made his heart heavy. Neither feeling was familiar to him. He made difficult rulings for his people every day, but he hoped he'd never misjudged a situation as badly as he had today.

Lamira stilled in his arms, her body growing heavy.

He watched her eyelids slide shut. "I asked for something to ease her pain, not put her out." He ought to be kinder to Daneth, who had been wise enough to seek the truth and brave enough to show it to him.

Daneth studied her readouts. "She may have been exhausted—stress will do that to a human." The physician glanced at the tray of food beside the sleeping platform. "She never ate?"

He shook his head miserably. "She said she was too upset."

"She will eat in the morning."

Heaviness overtook him. He needed to make amends to his delicate little human. Why hadn't she asked him for anything? He would have made her any gift, though she'd never shown much interest in his wealth or finery. And then he remembered what she did care for. "I want you to purchase her mother. She lived on the same agrifarm where you bought Lamira. Can you arrange it?"

Daneth bowed. "Of course, my lord."

"Has Seke seen the files?"

"Yes, my lord."

"Thank you, Daneth. That is all."

He waited until Daneth left, then said, "Call Seke."

When Seke's hologram popped up, the master at arms inclined his head to show respect, but said nothing. Because Seke was his teacher of battle arts, he did not grovel as much as the others did.

"You watched it?"

"I saw." Seke was a male of few words.

"There are no other data files of the two of them?"

"No, they are the only ones."

"Check on something else for me. Lamira said Gunt has been stealing crystals from the pod. I don't know how she would know such a thing, but I'd like you to investigate before I address Gunt."

"I'll investigate."

"Thank you." He flicked the hologram off and sighed, looking at his lovely slave. He had just flicked off the artificial light when her lids fluttered open and she blinked unfocused eyes.

"You're awake."

"Mmm." She smiled. The light of the giant Ocretion moon shone through the skylight, amplified by his crystal. It gave her a beautiful, bluish glow.

"You must feel better."

She rubbed her cheek on his chest, creating a riot of sensation everywhere she touched him. "I do."

"No more pain?"

Her cute freckled nose wrinkled. "Not much. And I feel happy." Her smile widened.

He'd never seen such a glorious sight. It made him want to work for that smile every minute of every planet rotation.

She reached for his horns.

He choked on a groan, and his cock surged to attention. She ran her dainty fingers around the width of one horn, rubbing it until it grew stiff, then she shifted her attention to the second horn. "Lamira," he choked, doing his best not to throw her on her back and pound her with his cock for a third time that planet rotation. "I don't think you know what you're doing."

Her smile grew naughty. "Oh, I think I do."

Zandian moons. She was smarter than he gave her credit for. He had underestimated her from the start, and now the entire fabric of his existence was unraveling beneath him as their dynamic shifted into something new.

He raised his eyebrows. "You *want* me to breed you again?" This time he was the one trembling from need.

She pushed herself up to her knees and straddled his waist, placing the heat of her pussy directly over his clothed cock. When she took hold of both horns, a shudder ran through him. All Zandian moons, when had she gained such control over his body?

He shoved his pants down and she climbed on, her naked body glowing in the moonlight.

She brought her lips to his and they were sugar-sweet, soft and—he groaned and gripped the back of her head to dominate the kiss, taking over, thrusting his tongue between her lips and nipping her.

She rocked her pelvis, taking his cock deeper into her glorious channel.

"Lamira..." He gripped her hips, careful not to touch her welted bottom, and helped her ride him, lifting and lowering her over his cock.

Soft tendrils of her hair fell against his neck, shocking his skin with the new sensation. Her intoxicating scent filled his nostrils.

He tilted his head to suck one of her beaded nipples then lost his concentration when she moaned, low and lusty.

"*Veck*, Lamira, *veck*."

She gave a keening cry, her inner thighs clamping around his hips, her lush ass undulating, breasts bouncing.

He wanted it to last forever, but the urge to drive to the finish took over. "On your hands and knees," he barked.

Her unfocused eyes blinked slowly, as if she were too dazed to comply, so he helped her, lifting her off him and pushing her down the way he wanted her.

He entered her, gripped her hips and pumped, forgetting to be gentle with her swollen bottom, slamming his loins against it.

Her tight pussy squeezed him like a glove, and she lifted her hips back to meet him. *Oh moons, oh yes.* His thighs tightened; cum surged down his shaft. He yanked her back against him, buried to the hilt, and shot his load into her canal.

She tightened around him, a good little slave, always waiting for his climax before she went off.

"Good girl," he purred, reaching around to stroke her little button and prolong her spectacular finish.

He set off a fresh wave of squeezing and her knees collapsed beneath her, sending both their hips to the sleepdisk, still connected.

"Good little slave," he murmured, biting her neck. "You took my cock three times in one day without complaining."

Not that she'd complained much if at all after the initial deflowering. No, she was a willing breeder—a perfect slave. A loyal slave. She hadn't given herself to Gunt, hadn't wanted anyone but him.

He bit the shell of her ear. "I'm sorry I punished you, Lamira," he murmured in her ear. "I wish I could take it back."

She turned her face to the side and laid her cheek on the sleeping platform, her eyes soft, face relaxed, as if thoroughly satiated. "I'm going to have your baby."

He stilled. "I beg your pardon?"

Her eyes snapped to focus and she shook her head as if shaking off her dreamy state. "I meant someday. Never mind."

He stroked a lock of copper hair behind her ear. As usual, he didn't understand his little human. They spoke the same language, but her words didn't make sense to him. It didn't matter. They had enough for now. He eased them both to their sides, his cock still inside her. He stroked slowly in and out of her, to savor the sensation.

Lamira emitted a contented sound and pulled his arm around her, bringing it to her breast. With a soft sigh, her eyelids slid closed again.

He wrapped his longer body around hers a curious sense of well-being flowing through him. Was it happiness? Did this little human make him happy?

If only they could learn to communicate. If only he could trust her.

~.~

Her dreams were full of Zander. Zander angry, gripping the horrible strap. Only this time she wasn't scared. *You're mine,* he said. *Mine alone. I will not share you.*

Yes, master. She dropped to her knees and reached for his cock.

Then Zander was buried inside her, murmuring in her ear. Zander fighting with Master Seke, his beautiful muscles rippling, his movement graceful like poetry.

She woke on an empty platform. She sat up. Zander's clothes and gold arm cuff lay on the sleepdisk and the sound of water rushed from the washroom.

She reached for the cuff. On the agrifarm, the foremen had used handheld communication devices. Zander's was state of the art, sleek and beautiful. As a human, she'd never been permitted to use any kind of device, but she'd looked over plenty of shoulders to see how they worked. In fact, she'd longed for one. She had a list a light-year long of the things she'd like to research. But they were mostly farming related. What would she search now, if she could?

Something about her new situation. Something to help her understand Zander better.

"Search Zandian Genocide."

Nothing happened. Right. Because they were programmed only for voice recognition. She remembered, once, seeing someone borrow a device.

"Guest user."

A light flickered on.

"Search Zandian Genocide."

A hologram hovered, showing images of airships bombing the capital of Zandia, Zandians running and screaming from burning buildings. A dispassionate voice over gave the facts of the date, which had been nearly twelve revolutions around the sun ago.

She realized she had something more important to research. With a trace of excitement, she said, "Search Leora Taniaka."

A hologram of her mother appeared, with the name of the agrifarm where they worked beneath it.

Well, at least nothing had changed.

"Search Lily Taniaka."

Her mother had asked every underground rebel for word of her sister for as long as she could remember.

A hologram of a young woman much like her popped up. The words underneath read, "Escaped slave. Whereabouts unknown." Her heart leapt. So her sister had escaped. Good for her. Perhaps she was part of the revolution, like their father.

The water in the washtube turned off.

"Close."

The hologram went on with the projection.

"Off. End." Her voice rose in pitch. How did she turn this thing off? Zander would kill her for using it!

"Stop. Over. Shut down. Close."

She clamped her hand over the light projecting the hologram.

The door to the washroom opened.

She tossed the cuff back where she found it, praying it had turned off.

Zander stepped out, fully naked. He seemed even larger without clothes—not only his cock—every part of him. His muscles bulged and rippled, from his wide shoulders and glorious pecs, to his washboard abs and sculpted thighs and calves. His skin glowed with the beautiful lavender tinge. And yes...his cock. It was huge even in repose, although it twitched to life as his violet eyes came to rest on her.

Her pussy clenched.

"You're awake."

"Yes, my lord."

She scrambled off the sleepdisk and stood to face him, the way he expected. As always, she was naked, except for the soft leather cuffs around her wrists, ankles and neck.

"Come here." He pulled fresh clothing from a shelf and put it on as she crossed the room to where he stood. When he finished dressing, he grasped her nape and pulled her up close to his face. To her shock, he planted a kiss on her forehead and released her. He walked to the sleepdisk and picked up his cuff.

As he fingered it, his head whipped around, eyes narrowed.

Veck. It must be warm, still. Or was a light on?

"Show last."

The hologram of her sister sprang up. He stretched it, looking from Lily's face back to hers. "Who is this? A sister?"

She wrung her fingers and nodded. "Yes," she managed to say. "I've never met her. She was taken from my parents for the sex trade when she was three."

Zander winced. "I'm sorry." His voice held a note of shock that made her believe him.

"Back."

The image of her mother hovered. He spun it around. "Is this your mother?"

"Yes, my lord."

"Back."

The first hologram she'd watched sprang up, right where it had left off, the disembodied voice explaining all the critical data points of what was probably the worst day in Zander's life.

She cringed.

"Back."

The hologram switched to a list of transactions—one of Zander's business accounting records.

"Close."

Her legs trembled when he swiveled his dark-eyed gaze on her. For a long, nerve-wracking moment, he said nothing, simply gazed at her speculatively. "What were you doing?"

It wasn't only her legs trembling. Her whole body shook. She didn't like Zander's dissatisfaction. She opened her jaw to keep her teeth from chattering. "I'm sorry."

He didn't move. Didn't speak.

Right. *I'm sorry* wasn't exactly an answer to his question, was it? For once, she tried for the truth. "I just wanted to understand you better."

He cocked an eyebrow. Once more, he made her suffer with a moment of silence. At last, he said, "Do not touch my things without permission."

She held her breath and waited to hear what the punishment would be. Her poor bottom couldn't take another thrashing, but the cage was almost worse.

He scrolled back to the Zandian invasion and zoomed in. His brow furrowed. "I've never seen this footage." His voice sounded hollow. She sensed the trauma beneath the words.

An image of him as a teenager, being hustled out to an airship flashed in her mind.

"How did you get away?"

He swallowed and rotated the rolling pictures, narrowing in on what must be the palace—his former home. "Master Seke evacuated the palace. He brought most of the servants...and me."

"The servants who are still here?"

"Yes."

She reached out to touch his arm. "I'm sure you wanted to stay and fight."

He turned his amethyst eyes on her, wide with wonder. "Exactly. My parents stayed to fight—both of them. I wanted to stay and fight, too, but they made me go with Seke—" He stopped speaking, his voice choked. "Everyone left on Zandia died that day."

"How many ships got away?"

He shook his head. "Only mine. The rest of the Zandians still alive today were away from the planet for the invasion. Lium and Erick. They were both offplanet."

"You're planning to take it back." She shouldn't have spoken. That was her claircognizance feeding her information she shouldn't know.

But Zander answered. "I *will* win it back." His jaw tightened with determination. "Release cuffs." The locks on her binds snapped open and the cuffs dropped to the floor. He jerked his head toward the washroom. "Go and wash. I have things to do."

She dipped into a curtsy, her heart aching for him. It was a huge responsibility he carried on his shoulders— the liberation of his people, the rightful return of his planet. No wonder he didn't have time for her.

She scooted off to the washroom and stepped into the washtube. The glorious washtube, which she'd come to love. She'd wash three times a day if she thought Zander would allow it. She stood under the warm spray and closed her eyes, allowing it to clean her. The water felt too warm on her still-sore bottom, but she didn't mind. Standing in that tube felt luxurious, indulgent, decadent. She held her breath as the water filled to the top then drained away and the warm air dried her.

She stepped out and combed her hair.

When she emerged from the washroom, Zander snapped her cuffs back in place. "Get in your cage. Today is the pod's recharge day."

She stared at him blankly.

"Once every ten planet rotations, Zandians must bathe in the light and eat a meal to maintain strength. On visitor's day, we open the light bath for outside Zandians. Today is the day those living here recharge. I'm going to the light bath now."

"Can't I come?" It wasn't only desperation at not being left in the cage—well, perhaps it was. But she also wanted to see the light baths and how they worked. She remembered the vision she'd had of the rainbow light and the joy spreading through her.

His dark gaze was unfathomable. Once more he stared at her a long time without speaking. Although she'd never been one to beg, she adopted a hopeful, expectant look.

He sighed and lifted his arm with the gold band. "Call Daneth." When Daneth's head popped up, he asked, "Is it safe for Lamira to enter the light bath?"

Daneth blinked a few times.

She stepped behind Zander to hide her nudity and peeked around his shoulder.

"I honestly cannot say for certain, my lord. I would think yes, so long as she wore protective eyewear. I do not know how well human eyes would withstand the light."

"Thank you." He hit something on the band and Daneth disappeared. "Put some clothes on."

She beamed at him, hurrying to dress. "Thank you, my lord," she said breathlessly.

"Let's go." He pressed his palm to the door.

"My lord." She ran to catch up with him and was startled when he took her hand in his as they walked swiftly down the corridor. She noticed Gunt had been replaced with a different guard. "You do not have to put me in the cage every time you leave your chamber. If you trust me enough to walk about the pod on my own, why not to stay in a room I cannot exit, which is guarded at all times?"

"Cage time is good for you." His deep voice sounded gruff, but rather than frighten her, it reverberated right in her core.

"Why?" she demanded.

"Research says once cage-trained, humans love them. It becomes a safe space. I like it because it reminds you of your place. Makes you happy to see me when I return."

Her pussy moistened and something slithered in her belly. Why? Surely she didn't *like* being trained like a pet by Zander?

He stepped up to a room she hadn't been in before and pressed his hand to the seal. It slid open. "Close your eyes."

She gasped when they stepped inside. A gigantic crystal had been installed in the ceiling, sending rainbow shafts of light all around the dome-shaped room.

"I said, *close your eyes*," Zander snapped.

She covered them with her palm and allowed him to lead her to the center of the room, where she'd seen narrow flat beds arranged in a circular pattern to match the shape of the room.

"Take off your clothes."

She pulled off her clothing and peeked to see him shucking his clothes as well. He guided her into a bed and she heard him settle in one next to her.

"Here," he said, dropping a piece of clothing over her face. His shirt, she thought. It smelled of his clean, masculine scent—a scent she'd come to love.

She breathed in deeply.

"Keep your face covered, just in case. I'd feel terrible if it got burned."

He'd feel terrible. So he must care about her. Or at least he took responsibility for her. Were they the same thing? Not necessarily.

She lay under the great crystal and paid attention to the sensations dancing across her skin. There was a tickling—no, a vibration. A humming of energy that made the hairs on her arms stand up. As the room grew quiet, a whisper became apparent.

King Zander will restore us to our planet. He needs you. Pay attention to all knowing.

She sat bolt upright and opened her eyes.

Zander's lids flew open and he glared at her. He pointed to the door, "*Out.*"

She snatched up the shirt and lay back down, covering her face again. "No, no. I'll be good. I'm sorry."

Her heart pounded against her ribs. No one was in the room but the two of them. Even as her rational brain struggled to answer the riddle, she already knew—the crystal had spoken to her. The *vecking* crystal.

Something about the experience made her weep. There was a lightness, a benevolence projecting from the crystal. Love, in its purest form. She felt grateful to be in its presence, grateful to be spoken to, to be needed by Zander.

Except...no. She couldn't tell Zander. Clearly he hadn't heard anything. Zandians, like humans, weren't supposed to just "know" things. Or "hear" things. Or "see" things. And while it may not be a trait punishable by death for a Zandian, it sure as hell was for a human.

So how would she help Zander with her knowing— the knowing that had never done her a bit of good in her life— when she couldn't reveal how she knew things?

Chapter Eight

"Gunt has stolen over thirty crystals from the pod in the last three solar cycles." Seke rubbed his forehead, his mouth turned down in disgust. "He sells them to Ocretions for a tidy sum. I'm sorry I didn't catch it."

"Where is he now?"

"He's in a holding cell."

Zander sighed. One of the downfalls of being part of a nearly extinct species was that he couldn't ever cut any being loose. He'd love to banish Gunt, but he didn't want to lose or waste any Zandian life.

"Leave him there. What else did you find? How did my human know?"

Zeke shook his head. "There's no other recording of the two of them, but I told you that before. There's no recording of her seeing him take them—they were all taken and sold before she got here."

Tension ran up Zander's shoulders to his neck. Something tight in his stomach made him feel sick. "But how could she know?" His voice rasped a little. "She was an agri-slave before she came here."

Zandian moons was she not a slave? Was she some kind of plant—perhaps part of the Finns' plot to kill him? But that would mean Daneth was part of it. Or someone had tampered with his program...

Seke's eyes narrowed, and he knew the older man had the same thoughts. He was the one who had taught Zander the art of war and strategy, after all. "I don't know."

Zander stood up. "I'll question her."

Turmoil swirled through his insides as he stalked back to his chamber where he'd left Lamira out of her cage. He wouldn't make that mistake again.

He opened the door and let it close behind him. Lamira scrambled off the bed to stand before him, naked, as he required. Her beauty angered him now. Was she an elaborate ploy to get close to him? If so, to what end? And how dangerous could she be? He could snap her neck with the flick of a hand.

He stared at her for a moment and watched her fidget. "How did you know about Gunt and the crystals?"

Genuine fear flashed across her face—her pupils narrowed, breath shortened. He smelled it coming from her pores.

It chilled him. So she did have something to hide.

She shook her head quickly and took a step back. "I didn't. It was a guess, that's all. Was I right?"

"Come here."

Something twitched in her cheek. She stepped closer to him.

He picked her up by the armpits and lifted her until they came eye to eye. "Do. Not. Lie to me." He kept his voice even and cold.

A shiver ran through her. It brought him some small satisfaction. Her reactions were so transparent. She couldn't be a spy. At least, not a trained agent. She was a terrible liar and while her emotions confused him, she wore them on the outside. Surely a spy—even a human one—would have more skill.

"Zander, please. I swear—I don't know anything."

"You knew about Gunt. How did you?"

"He didn't seem trustworthy, that's all."

Zander shook his head. "No. You told me he was stealing crystals. That's a specific accusation, and Master Seke has proven it to be true. So how did you know?"

His little slave looked beautiful with tears swimming in her eyes, lips trembling, a wide-eyed pleading look on her face, her naked body vulnerable and available to him. "I didn't know," she insisted, not quite meeting his eyes.

He dropped her back to her feet. "I promised you a whipping the next time you lied."

She blanched, her little hands reaching back to cover her still-marked ass. He should punish her again, but he couldn't bring himself to. Still, anger coursed through his body, much like it had the night before. Once more, this little human had completely thrown off his equilibrium.

"I punished you yesterday when you didn't deserve it, so I won't strap you again. But I am very angry with you. Kneel at my feet and do not speak—I do not wish to hear your voice."

He turned away from her, taking a seat at his work platform, but his mind was on nothing but the docile, delicate creature at his feet. When had she become so submissive? Had he already tamed her in a short week? How?

She sniffed, and he smelled the scent of her salty tears.

"Why are you crying? I haven't caused you pain. Yet."

"I'm not crying."

He grabbed her hair and yanked her head back. "You continue to lie when evidence of the truth is right here on your face?" He flicked his tongue to catch the salty drop.

She jerked her head away. "Stupid master. I'm not"—she huffed out a sigh—"the words weren't intended to deceive."

He let the *stupid master* part slide, only because her face crinkled with distress. "Oh, right, they are what you wish were true. If you do not wish to cry, do not. Is it so hard for you?"

She jerked away. "Yes."

He picked her up and arranged her on his lap, gripping her face to turn it toward him. "Why do you cry?"

The tears continued to swim in her eyes. "I don't like displeasing you."

His eyebrows slammed down. "If you do not like displeasing me, then don't," he thundered, the deep tones of his voice reverberating against the walls.

She flinched, shrinking back from him.

He remembered that he'd truly frightened her the last time. But shouldn't a slave be afraid of her master when she disobeys?

"Tell me the truth."

Again real fear flashed in her eyes. What was she hiding?

"Come here." He pulled her up by her arm and marched her to the spanking bench Daneth had provided. With a shove, he positioned her over it and snapped her cuffs to lock her in place.

"Zander...Zander, please. I didn't know. I don't know anything."

"Stop the lies." He slapped her upturned ass, and she shrieked. After rooting through the box of implements, he found the butt plug and ginger oil to make it burn. He coated the plug in the oil and pressed the tip against her little rosette. "I won't whip you, but you deserve to feel my dissatisfaction, slave."

She squeezed her butt cheeks together to keep him out.

"Open up, or I will change my mind about spanking you."

"Zander..." Her voice shook.

His armband flashed her readout: *Forty percent aroused.* "Now."

One cheek relaxed then the other. He rubbed the bulbous head of the butt plug over her anus and waited for the sphincter muscles to relax. The moment they did, he pushed the object inside, stretching her slowly.

"No," she cried out. "Ah!"

Seventy percent aroused.

"Bad slave." He eased the plug in farther, and she squealed at the largest part. She took the entire plug into her cavity, her anus closing around the narrow neck, leaving the steel handle protruding.

Ninety-five percent aroused.

He pumped it a few times, the sounds of alarm she made turning his cock rock hard. She tightened around the plug.

Climax achieved.

"Did you come?" he snapped. "Bad slave. You do not orgasm without my cock inside you—without my seed inside you." He spanked her with his hand, the plug jostling as she bucked.

One hundred percent aroused.

He unclipped her from the bench and fastened her wrists behind her back. With a tug, he pulled her to sit on his lap on the sleeping platform, facing away from him. He pinched both her nipples. She threw herself back against him, arching and writhing. He spread her knees so wide they hooked over his, leaving her pussy exposed and vulnerable. With a snap of his wrist, he spanked her wet pussy, his fingers slapping again and again to punish her.

Climax approaching.

"Oh! Oh please. Oh wait—stop—Zander! No... Oh no, I'm going to do it again—"

He shoved his pants down and lifted her onto his cock. She slid on easily, her passageway swollen and wet, more than ready for him. He lifted and lowered her over his cock, the end of the butt plug connecting with his pelvis and shoving it in deeper on each instroke.

Lamira babbled something—nonsense mostly, her gasps and cries one long string of sound.

He moved her just the way he wanted her—grinding over his cock, her back arching and breasts thrusting in the air. He bounced her up and down until he couldn't hold back any longer. Yanking her in, he climaxed, shooting his load. It only took one tap of his finger against her clitoris and his little human came, too, her muscles squeezing his cock, massaging it, milking it for his seed.

Climax achieved.

Since she was still being punished, he didn't cuddle her afterward, but lifted her up and placed her on the sleepdisk, with her ankles strung up in the air, holding her hips aloft.

Ninety-five percent aroused.

Still? Well, so was he.

Somehow, punishment had turned into a glorious game. Yes, he was still annoyed with her, but not enough not to enjoy her luscious body. She looked unbelievably hot strung up like that. He adjusted one of her ankles so her legs were spread wide. The view of her pussy was spectacular. Swollen, glossy, with traces of rainbow colors from his seed. He brought his hand down between her legs and spanked her swollen folds again.

~.~

She couldn't help it. She climaxed again, the moment he slapped her sex.

Of course, there was no hiding it, with his cuff giving off constant data on the state of her vagina.

He slapped her clenching pussy again. "What did I say about orgasming without my cock inside you?"

She couldn't muster any intelligible reply. "Ugn...uh..."

"I will let it slide, since my seed is already planted."

She couldn't decide if he was playing with her or was genuinely still angry. The line had grown blurry during sex. She feared he had come to understand his dominance aroused her. She hadn't yet admitted it to herself, even, but his damn arm cuff didn't lie.

"You will remain in this position for thirty minutes." He set a timer on his cuff and turned away.

She sighed. The position left her still impossibly aroused, despite the multiple orgasms. She prayed no one entered the chamber to see her like that.

Zander worked at his platform while she tried to cool her engines.

The ankle cuffs began to cut into her flesh and her feet went numb. She shifted around, but there was little she could do in the ridiculous position.

Zander turned his violet gaze on her. He didn't seem angry.

"Please, my lord. My feet have lost all feeling."

He stood and sauntered over, grasping one of her feet. She gasped as pins and needles shot through when he touched it. With a quick command, he released the clips on her ankles and scooped her into his arms, carrying her to his sitting platform where he sank back down with her cradled in his lap.

This. Yes. Stars, yes. She loved when he held her afterward. She rubbed her feet together, tensing at the sensation returning to them.

He looked down at her and tweaked one nipple between his thumb and forefinger. "I like when you look at me like that."

She hardly dared breathe. Was Zander actually paying her a compliment? "How do I look?" She spoke softly, not wishing to jar Zander out of his unusual tenderness.

He smirked. "Like I'm your entire universe."

"Well," she said lightly, "you *are* my master."

His eyes narrowed as if trying to determine if she was being sarcastic. For once, she wasn't. She'd meant what she said. He was her master. In the short time she'd been with him, he had become her entire world. Bending to his will meant avoiding punishment, and even earning comfort. So, yes, he had become her entire universe.

"Lamira, you must tell me the truth now."

All the post-climactic languor fled her body in a single moment. She stiffened in his arms, attempting to sit upright. He didn't allow it. "Don't lie again."

She blinked up at him. She wanted to obey. But how could she? It would mean her death.

"Are you really from an agrifarm?"

"Yes, my lord. I swear it." She met his unbelieving eyes.

How could she prove her innocence?

"I can show you the plants I've started in your great hall," she offered. She'd been dying to show him her work but had made herself wait until more had sprouted.

He lifted her to her feet, his lips pursed. "All right. Show me."

She turned big pleading eyes on him. "Take the plug out? Please, my lord?" It still burned, heating her pelvis from the inside out.

"No." His voice had the hard edge to it. He had not forgiven her, no matter what gentleness he'd shown after sex.

"You're still angry."

He nodded. "Yes. I don't see the point of keeping a slave I cannot trust."

She stopped on her way to put on her clothes, a chill running through her. "Zander," she breathed, her vision blurring.

Would he send her back? The thought of returning to the agrifarm, even to her mother, left her empty. That wasn't where she belonged. The crystals had spoken to her. She'd seen the baby.

That's right, she'd seen the baby. He wouldn't send her away. She'd prove her innocence to him. She yanked on her clothing and drew herself up, her head held high.

~.~

Lamira chattered on about her plants, using the Latin Earth names for the little sprouts. The glow on her face nearly matched the sunlight pouring in through the crystals, shining through her coppery hair in shimmering waves.

She walked stiffly, the plug in her ass plainly causing her discomfort, the flush on her face as clear a readout as the one on his cuff.

He liked her aroused. Maybe he'd keep her that way all day until she confessed her secret. It was hard to believe she was a spy. She wasn't good enough at it. But why wouldn't she tell him how she knew about Gunt stealing crystals?

"So you see? Soon we'll have fresh food grown here. The plants love your crystal light—it's amazing how quickly the seedlings have grown. Three times as fast as they would've on the agrifarm. I only wish I had more space. I'd love to have an entire room of raised beds to work with."

He steeled himself against her beauty, against the way his lips fought to reward her excitement with a smile. The more he was around her, the more discombobulated he became. This human was trouble for him.

He gripped her elbow. "It's time for your ass-*vecking*."

Her green eyes flew wide and the color drained from her face. "But, my lord..."

"Unless you're ready to tell me how you knew about Gunt?"

Her expression clouded, worry gathering on her brow.

"Let's go." He tugged her back down the hall, the thought of taking her ass putting a spring into his step.

Perhaps their impasse did not have to be unpleasant. He certainly enjoyed punishing his little slave.

He led her to his chamber and propelled her into the washroom. "Clothes off."

Like an obedient breeder, she stripped, folding her clothes neatly and stacking them in a pile on the counter. She seemed eager to appease him. He could get used to having her around. And that was cause for concern. Because, right now, he should be focused on winning the battle for Zandia.

"Bend over the counter." He spun her around and pushed her torso down on the cool stone surface. Daneth had given him equipment to clean her bowels, and he pulled it out now, attaching one end of the hose to the water line from the sink and filling the water bag.

The handle of the oiled plug nested between her pretty cheeks, giving evidence to her humiliation. She'd be getting an even larger dose now. He eased the plug out of her hole, smiling at her gasp.

"Reach back and hold your cheeks open for me."

"Why?"

He slapped her ass. "Really, little slave? You're going to question me?"

"No, my lord," she mumbled. He met her eyes in the mirror and saw anguished surrender.

Beautiful.

"Open them wide."

"Yes, my lord." She reached back and peeled her lovely cheeks wide, exposing the delicate pink rosebud of her anus.

He rubbed a lubricant—not the ginger kind this time—on the top of the nozzle and inserted it into her anus.

Her gasp of alarm made his cock hard.

He opened the clamp and let the water fill her bowels.

She moaned. "Please, my lord. What are you doing? Please don't..."

He liked her begging.

The bag emptied.

"I'm cleaning you out for me. I need you to hold that water until I say you can let it go."

"I can't," she moaned. "Please, my lord."

"Tell me how you knew about Gunt."

Silence.

"Are you a spy?"

"No, no, no, no," she breathed, her self-control clearly challenged by holding the water inside her. "Not a spy. It was a lucky guess."

"Don't insult me with your lies."

"Please," she whined. "I can't hold it any longer."

"Two more minutes."

"I can't..."

"You will."

He smelled the salty scent of her tears. For a moment, he regretted pushing her, but then he remembered her lies.

She shifted from foot to foot, her anus visibly clenching in spasms around the tube still inserted in her ass. At last, he removed it. "Empty yourself for your ass-*vecking*." He left her alone in the washroom to finish up.

She emerged, subdued and pale.

"On the sleeping platform, on your knees and forearms. Ass in the air."

She crawled up to the platform and assumed the position. "Spread your knees wider."

She obeyed. The lips of her sex parted wide, swollen and wet.

He ran his finger lightly over her slit, smiling when her entire body shuddered. "What happens to slaves who lie to their masters?"

"I-I don't know," she whispered.

He rubbed his finger over her clitoris, feeling it swell and harden under his fingertip.

"They get their asses *vecked*. Hard. Is that what you want?"

He spread her glossy juices up to her clit.

She made an unintelligible sound.

"Bad slave." He released his cock from his trousers and rubbed lubricant over it. "You have displeased your master."

"Forgive me," she panted, sounding breathless.

He fit a large vibrating dildo in her cunt and flicked it on.

She gave a startled, wanton cry.

"Hold still," he commanded and pushed the head of his cock against her anus, waiting until the tight ring of muscle relaxed and allowed him entry.

Her moans sounded alarmed.

Despite his purpose in punishing her, he experienced a rush of affection. To take his large Zandian cock in her tight ass asked a lot. Her humbled position endeared her to him. From his point of view, her bottom splayed wide, her cunt dripping, her ass taking his cock like a good slave, she was *vecking* gorgeous. He slid in and out, loving the tightness.

"Bad little slave," he murmured, but his tone sounded affectionate. He couldn't help it—he loved taking her like this, loved owning her so completely.

He turned up the speed on the vibrating wand in her twat and pumped harder.

She wailed beneath him, her cries rising to a keening pitch. "Please, master, please. I'm sorry. I'll be a good slave. I swear I'll be a good slave."

His balls tightened. He shot his load, wasting his seed in her ass. It had been worth it. Euphoric victory coursed through his veins.

He eased out of his slave's ass and turned off the vibrator. "You didn't climax," he murmured, gathering Lamira up in his arms.

"No, but it feels like I did." Her lips barely moved. Her body lay limp and spent in his arms. A sheen of sweat gave her skin a glow.

Beautiful.

He wanted to give her the world. He couldn't wait for her mother to arrive.

He wished they were not at an impasse over her lies.

~.~

Zander punished her every planet rotation. During the days, he put her in the cage and left. She had a feeling he was training for war—his plans to take back his planet filtered into her consciousness daily. Since the crystal bath, her knowings had come more often, more clearly. She saw an image of her mother, dressed in luxurious robes, and rejoiced that she was still alive and would know freedom.

At night, he asked her if she was ready to tell him the truth. When she refused, he punished her. The first night he paddled her with a horrible wooden board. She sobbed and begged for his mercy, but, as usual, her traitorous body somehow became aroused at the punishment, ready for him to breed the moment the spanking ended.

The next night, he went easy on her, perhaps taking pity on her still-swollen ass. He spanked her with his hand and forced her to suck his cock until he came down her throat.

The third night, he used a terrible cane on her. That night, she'd wept so bitterly at the pain he had not bred her, instead he'd taken her into his arms on his sleepdisk, stroking her back and hair until she drifted off to sleep.

The fourth night, he used only his hand again.

She couldn't hate him. He took such care with her, even when he punished. It was odd, but while she feared the pain he liked to inflict, she wasn't afraid of him. Not the way she had been afraid of the guards at the agrifarm. Not even the way she was wary of Daneth, though he'd never hurt her.

She woke the following morning with her wrists chained over her head, Zander's hot hands roaming over her breasts.

She arched into them, shivers of excitement rolling through her. Her pussy, which was nearly perpetually wet since Zander had begun breeding her, heated and began to pulse.

"Little Lamira. You're such a bad slave."

No, I'm not. I'm your good slave.

Where did that come from? At what point had she started desiring his approval? Wanting to please him? Right from the beginning, it seemed.

He straddled her and brought his thumb and forefinger to one of her nipples, pinching it. "When are you going to stop lying to me?"

God, would he ever let it go?

Her eyes slid sideways, away from his amethyst gaze.

Slap. His palm swatted the side of her breast. She arched and yanked against her binding.

"Do I need to spank your breasts?" He slapped its twin.

"Oh! No..." She writhed beneath him, uselessly trying to twist away from him, to hide herself.

Despite the pain and what was worse—the fear at this new, untried form of punishment—moisture seeped onto her inner thigh. Her wanton pussy was ready for whatever her large master had to offer.

He slapped her breast one more time but then climbed off, his gaze decidedly cool. "No, I think I'll try something else today."

A fresh ripple of fear went through her and she shivered. "Master?"

"I will deny you my cock. You may have been reluctant to take it at first, but now I think you've grown to enjoy it...perhaps it is too much of a reward."

She ought to be relieved the punishment was so mild, but he was right—denying her his cock left her yearning. Empty. Rejected.

Shifting his tone into the quiet command he used on the electronics, he said, "Release cuffs."

She sat up, whimpering at the pain of the blood rushing fully into her arms.

Zander looked over his shoulder at her on his way to the washroom and she swore she saw a wrinkle of concern on his forehead. He hesitated but then shook his head and entered the washroom.

She flopped back on the sleepdisk and sighed. Living with her master presented a new torture every day. Not the kind she'd expected. No, the emotional kind. Longing and angst. Need, desire...and love? It made her stomach clench to think the word, but, yes, she'd certainly become emotionally attached. Bonded. Maybe it was love, maybe it wasn't. She really didn't know about these things.

Her stomach rumbled. She got up, dressed, and tapped on the washroom door. "Master? May I go to the kitchen to eat?"

"Yes." His answer was short and clipped. "But return in twenty minutes. I'm leaving for the United Galaxies meeting this morning, and you must stay in your cage while I'm gone.

Ugh. A long day alone in the cage. She'd hated the last few days. Servants brought her food and liquid and let her out for a walk and to use the washroom, but she hated staying cooped up. The only way she'd kept from going insane was paying attention to her claircognizance. Something she never used to do.

She walked down to the kitchen. "Good morning, Barr," she chirped. Seeing the friendly chef always cheered her.

He rewarded her with a broad smile. "Lamira. Guess what I made for you this morning?" He set a plate with a beautiful breakfast pie in front of her. "It's called quiche. Have you ever heard of it? It's a human recipe I researched."

She blinked back tears. "You researched human recipes?"

"Yes, from old Earth. I know you probably wouldn't know them, but I thought perhaps they'd be especially good for your body." He blushed after mentioning her body.

She smiled. "That was so thoughtful of you. What's in it?"

The older Zandian beamed. The crust is made with a flour and butter, the inside is egg, cream, cheese and vegetables. He waited with anticipation on his face, for her to take her first bite.

She picked up the utensil and popped a serving into her mouth. "Mmm...it's...absolutely delicious," she said, still chewing. "Thank you so much!"

Barr smiled. "My pleasure."

She ate quickly, partly to show Barr how much she loved it and partly because she didn't want to be late for her curfew. When she'd eaten every last crumb from the plate, she stood. "Thank you again. Really. I am touched by your efforts. You're wonderful, Barr."

His skin turned a darker purple and he ducked his head. "Have a good day, Lamira."

"You too, Barr."

She headed back to Zander's room, running down the hallway in case she was late.

Zander stood outside the door to his chamber, listening to Master Seke tell him something. Their heads were bent together and Zander's forehead wrinkled.

He threw her a distracted look and opened the door. "Go in your cage."

That was it? He was trusting her to go in the cage on her own. Her heart picked up speed as she contemplated disobedience. To be safe, she crawled up into the cage and swung the door mostly shut but stopped before the lock clicked into place. There. If he came in and secured it, that would be that. If not...would she dare leave it during the day? Would his servants know and report her?

Well, she could figure that out after he left.

She listened for the sound of the door opening, but it never came.

As always, she closed her eyes to shut out the closeness of the bars. An image immediately flooded her mind.

It showed Zander's ship docking somewhere—a huge complex—the United Galaxies headquarters, perhaps. The moment it arrived, the dock blew into smithereens.

She gulped for air.

No.

Oh stars, no. Zander.

Kicking open the cage, she scrambled out and ran for the door. For a moment, she feared Zander had locked it so she couldn't leave, but it slid open.

She raced down the hall, her bare feet digging into the luxurious rugs. Where would he be? Had he already gone? Remembering the direction of the dock from Gunt's tour, she charged through space.

There.

At the end of the corridor, surrounding by a group of guards and advisors, about to step out into the docking platform.

"Zander!" she screamed.

He whirled around, a frown creasing his brow.

Ah stars, what would she tell him? She couldn't say what she'd seen.

But she had to stop him—had to.

"What are you doing out of your cage?" he demanded.

"My lord—you can't go!"

She reached him and gripped his forearm, tugging at it. Of course, he was completely immovable. Her heart beat wildly in her chest, the image of the explosion still burning her eyes.

"What in the Zandian moons are you doing? Why aren't you in your cage?"

Under different circumstances, she'd be embarrassed that he mentioned her cage in front of other beings, but she didn't have time to care now. All that mattered was keeping him from getting on that ship.

"Zander—please don't go. You can't!" She probably sounded hysterical. Hell, she felt hysterical. "Please, my lord."

He gripped her shoulders and gave her a shake, like a naughty child. "What's wrong with you?"

She needed to give him some kind of reason. Her brain raced, searching for something, anything she could tell him that would make him stay. "Right now. I'm ovulating. You have to breed me. This is our one chance for the lunar cycle."

Yes, it was a stupid reason, but it was the first thing she could think of.

"I think the crystal bath kicked it into gear."

Zander's brow furrowed even further, but he shook her off his arm. "Go back to your cage, Lamira. *Now*. I have to get to the UG complex and I don't have time to waste with you today."

She grasped him again, holding his arm tight as he tried to tug it away, causing him to yank her forward and into the air. She twisted wildly as her feet grasped for purchase, refusing to let go of his forearm.

"*Lamira*." He shook his arm so hard, her teeth rattled. So much disapproval and irritation rang through in that single word, but she didn't care. If she let Zander go, he'd die. She'd seen it.

"You *cannot* go," she hissed.

His eyes blazed dark-purple. A muscle in his jaw tightened.

"This is unacceptable." The room tilted and flipped upside down as she found herself upended over Zander's shoulder. His hand clapped down on her ass, hard. "Start the engines. I will be there in a moment," he barked over his shoulder as he walked swiftly down the corridor.

Think, Lamira, think. There must be a way to convince him to stay. Something she could do or say?

Zander slapped her ass again, his irritation coming through clearly in the stinging blow.

She steeled herself against the continued spanks. If she'd known sooner, she might have disabled the ship. No, that was foolish. She didn't have the slightest clue how to disable a ship, even if she were able to get away with such a thing.

They arrived back in Zander's chambers, where he dropped her on her feet and glowered.

"Don't go," she whispered, her body trembling from her scalp to the tips of her toenails.

Zander put his hands on his hips. "What is this about? Is this because I denied you sex this morning?"

"No—" It was silly to keep the up the lie about her ovulation, but she hadn't come up with a better idea. "It's just now is our best chance—to conceive a baby. It has to be right now."

He glanced at his armband. "I do not have the time right now. I am the ambassador of my species, and I'm supposed to be at a United Galaxies meeting representing our interests *at this very moment*. Are you so foolish you cannot discern what is of the highest importance here?"

Tears of desperation leaked from the corners of her eyes. "Zander...you don't understand..."

He'd lost all patience with her, though, and stalked to the box of punishment tools. He withdrew the cane she hated with every particle of her being.

Well, at least it meant he was staying—if only for a few more minutes.

He grabbed her elbow and spun her around to face the sleeping platform. "Bend over, pants down."

Nothing could be more humiliating than folding her torso over the platform and reaching back to bare her own bottom for his punishment. She gritted her teeth, flinching when the cool air reached her butt cheeks.

The cane sliced through the air.

She cried out, rising onto her toes.

"That is for leaving your cage."

He whipped her again.

"Or did you never get into it?"

"I did, I did!" she cried out, as if that would stop the horrible cane from swinging again.

"Is that another one of your lies?" he demanded, the cane landing again.

"No, master! I was in it, but the door never locked!" *Because I didn't lock it.*

He laid another stripe across her twitching flesh.

Stars, it hurt.

"And that is for refusing to return when I ordered it." Two quick strikes.

She felt certain she was going to die.

"And this is for still arguing with me as if you might pester me into getting your way." Three more terrible strokes.

She sobbed into the sleepdisk covers.

He threw the cane on the sleeping platform. "Now get in that cage and stay there until I return."

No. She couldn't let him leave. She pushed herself weakly to her feet and turned, her pants tangling around her legs. "Don't go," she croaked. "You can't leave—please don't go."

He threw her a look of disgust and stalked out, the door whooshing closed behind him.

She stood there, tears streaking her face, her ass on fire, trying to think of something else she might do to keep him from that meeting. But nothing came. Her brain had frozen in fear, stopped cold with the vision of her master—her lover—exploding.

~.~

Zander drew deep breaths as his long, hurried strides carried him back to the ship dock. He'd thought Lamira was smarter than that. What in the stars had she been thinking? He ought to punish her again when he returned. No. He needed to talk to her, to try to understand why she felt so strongly about breeding with him today. Because surely she understood she risked punishment, and yet she did it anyway.

He glanced at his cuff. *Veck, veck veck.* He should be flying already. They'd assigned his ship a specific garage and dock time to cut down on air traffic problems, and now he'd be lucky if he made it by the end of the window. And he had planned to leave with plenty of time to spare. He hated being late. The UG required each ambassador to dock and remain in their docking area for security clearance. The entire process took at least an hour. If he missed his docking window, he might have to wait even longer to be allowed out of his docking garage and into the Great Hall.

His guards stood at the dock door, looking alert and ready. Master Seke also stood waiting. He would accompany Zander into the meeting and serve as his primary advisor and protector.

They folded in when he passed, following him onto the craft. He sat down in the pilot's chair, not because he didn't have staff who could fly but because he preferred to be the one in control. All the battle flight simulators in the galaxy didn't compare to actual flight. Not that the simple flight path to the UG was anything like a battle.

Seke took the co-pilot's chair. His expression was blank, as always. He wouldn't ask about Lamira, either. He was a being of few words.

"The human is disrupting everything," he complained. He knew he sounded like a petulant, spoiled little prince. She was his breeder. He should be able to handle her without whining to his advisors about it. Zander eased the craft out of the docking station and zipped onto the flight path at top speed. He needed to make up the time he'd spent with Lamira in his chamber.

Seke leaned back in his chair. "Yes, she has affected you."

That wasn't what he meant. What in the Zandian moons was Seke saying?

His aggravation level increased. The spacecraft wove in and out of traffic, maintaining speed.

"She's too big a distraction. I cannot go on—"

"Give it more time," Seke interrupted in his ever-calm voice. "We've never had a female living on the pod before. It's natural for adjustments to occur."

He gave his head a quick shake. Even now he was thinking about her when he should be focused on the assembly meeting.

He slowed the speed of the craft as the traffic grew heavier around the UG pod. Winding his way through the other airships, he circled to the back to his assigned docking station. He glanced at his cuff. One minute late. Hopefully they hadn't opened the inner doors yet.

He cut the engines completely and coasted in toward the dock.

White light exploded in front of them and, a second later, a boom deafened him.

"Cut away," Seke barked, unbuckling his harness.

He flicked the switch for the engines to fire back to life at the same time he wrenched the steering arm to the left. The craft banked, flying into flames.

For a moment, he thought they entire ship would explode—he'd flown too close to the source of the fire. But then the smoke and flames cleared and the craft circled away.

The moment they were free of the flames, Seke ran back to man the weaponry, barking orders at the guards. "Check for incoming."

"We have three on our tail, Master," one of the guards shouted back.

"Fire at will."

Laser fire lit up the windows.

Zander dodged the cluster of airships in his way, dropping down to lure the attacking ships into open territory where his crew could get a clear shot. It must be a Finnian attack.

A flash of light glared behind them as one ship exploded.

"Target one, destroyed," his guard reported.

"Target two acquired," Seke said, his voice still calm, even while the rest of the crew yelled.

Another explosion.

"Target two destroyed."

"Third target has fallen back."

He whipped the craft around. No way he was letting his enemy get away. Chasing the retreating fighter craft, he wove in and out of traffic, keeping his gaze locked on target three."

"A little closer, my lord."

He shoved the throttle open, hurtling forward through space.

"Target three acquired. And..."

Another ship darted into their path, and Zander yanked up to avoid a crash. *Veck.* He swung back around, but the fighter craft had disappeared.

"Where is it?" he shouted.

The area was too congested. Aircraft flew all around. The *vecking* enemy had slipped through their fingers.

Seke returned to the co-pilot's chair and sat down.

"I'm going back to the UG."

"Not advised. That was a trap, laid precisely for you. We must get you back to the pod and tighten security."

"I'm not running to hide like a terrified animal!"

"This is not the war. It was not even a battle. It was a plot to assassinate you before you have a chance to assemble your warriors. Do not give them an additional chance to kill you. Your species need you alive."

He gritted his teeth, but turned the craft and recharted for his pod.

"The bomb must have been set on a timer. If you had been on time, we all would have died."

Ice washed over his skin.

He remembered Lamira's wild eyes as she yanked at his arm. *My lord—you can't go.* She'd seemed desperate to stop him. *"She knew."* He glanced over at Seke, to see if the master warrior had arrived at the same conclusion.

"It seems so."

A heavy silence fell over them. How did she know? Was she part of this assassination plot? Had she been planted as an insider? Perhaps she'd fallen in love and changed her mind.

In love. The thought tore at his heart.

She'd saved his life and he'd whipped her for her troubles.

But who was she? A stone sank to the pit of his stomach. He could never trust this human. Not even if he kept her locked up in a cage for the rest of her life. There were too many unknowns about her unusual knowledge, and too many beings who wanted him dead.

~.~

Lamira jerked awake to the sound of voices in the corridor. She shifted in the cage and gasped at the pain still radiating from her ass. Worse was the incredible tightness in her chest, the heaviness of lead weighing it down.

Zander. Her Zander. Was he already dead? Some part of her wailed inside in mourning.

The door slid open.

Was it already lunchtime?

She twisted and her breath caught.

"Zander!"

Her master looked pale, but unharmed. His haunted gaze raked over her.

"Open cage."

She scrambled out and he caught her and lifted her down, but his brows were drawn together, as if disturbed.

"Zander, are you all right?"

"You knew." His voice cracked.

She reached out to touch his face, still overjoyed to see him alive.

He caught her wrist but allowed the touch, pressing her hand to his cheek. "Were you trying to save me?"

If her emotions were not so wrecked from fear and then joy, she would have played it differently. She would have played ignorant. But his drawn expression made her worry—perhaps his crew had died.

"A-are you all right? Was anyone hurt?"

"Who set the bomb? How are you connected to them?" The lash of his cold voice whipped her.

She jerked her hand away, realizing her colossal mistake. Shaking her head, she backed away. "No...I don't know anything."

"Enough with your lies!" He lunged forward and caught her by the throat, lifting her from the floor and squeezing until her breath died.

She kicked and clawed at his fingers, her eyes bugging out in panic.

As if he suddenly realized he might kill her, he dropped her, pain etched in the deepened lines on his forehead.

She coughed, rubbing her throat.

He stood staring at her, his fingers clenching and unclenching in fists. Were those tears swimming in his eyes?

The sight of him, so reduced from her deceit, made her abandon her pretense and speak more directly. "I'm not working with your enemies—I swear to you, Zander. I have no connections. But I can't tell you how I knew or it could mean my life."

"You are safe here," Zander roared, the muscles bulging in his neck and shoulders as he took a step forward. When she flinched backward, he stopped himself and didn't touch her. Perhaps he was afraid he might kill her. He jabbed his chest. "I will protect you. My enemies won't touch you here."

"It's not your enemies. You wouldn't even believe me, if I told you the truth. I just—I can't tell you."

He stepped closer and grasped the hair at the back of her head, tipping her head back. His face drew very close to hers, his beautiful eyes light-purple. "You must tell me," he whispered hoarsely, his lips centimeters from hers, his gaze so intent, she thought she'd dissolve into a puddle.

She blinked back at him, her knees weak and wobbly, her breath stalled in her chest. "I can't," she finally managed to say.

She expected anger, but instead Zander closed his eyes. He released her hair and cradled her face, bringing his forehead to touch hers. When his lids blinked open, she was certain she saw excess moisture there.

"Lamira—" he began, his throat catching. "You saved my life and for that, I will make sure you live out your life in peace."

Her heart missed a beat as it roared to a gallop, thudding painfully against her sternum. Was he getting rid of her? "Zander—" she cried in protest.

"Shh." He tightened his grip on her face, covering her ears with his large palms. "I...I cannot go on this way." His voice choked. "I can't keep you near me when you cannot be trusted." He thumbed away a tear she didn't realize she'd cried. "I know you care about me. I saw your distress this morning when you thought I would die. I care about you, too. More than I would like to admit." His forehead wrinkled. "Is this what you humans call love?"

Love. Was it? Stars, yes. She loved this being with all her heart, despite her position as his slave and breeder.

She nodded, fresh tears streaming down her face.

He mopped them with his thumbs. Tilting his head down, he crushed his lips to hers, licking and sucking, demanding her kiss roughly.

She gave it to him, hoping—praying it didn't mean what she thought it did.

Good-bye.

But it did. When he broke away, he raised his voice and called to Herman, the guard who had replaced Gunt outside his door. "Take Lamira and her things to a guest chamber."

"Of course, my lord." Herman flicked a curious glance at her.

She pointed weakly at the shelf where her clothing lay stacked in neat piles. "Those are my only things."

Herman scooped them up and led the way out the door.

"Zander..." Her voice broke. "Please don't do this."

"Go, Lamira. It's not safe for me to be around you."

She choked back a sob and turned to follow Herman, her head bowed in surrender.

This could not be how things ended. She would find a way to prove her trustworthiness to Zander again.

~.~

Zander pulled off his boot and hurled it against the wall. The clunk was not nearly as satisfying as he'd hoped, but he repeated the action with the second boot anyway.

Why?

What did all this mean? His beautiful Lamira...his slave. A spy? How was she tangled up in the political machinations of the Galaxy? What connections did she have that gave her such underground knowledge—information none of his spies had discovered?

He sank down on the sleeping platform and rubbed his face.

He should send her away—far away.

But how would he live without her?

Chapter Nine

Zander leaned his head in his hands at his work platform. He couldn't think. Or, rather, couldn't focus on the work at hand. All he thought about was the youthful human female locked in his guest quarters.

He'd hadn't risked seeing her—he knew where it would lead. Straight to pushing her down and spreading those long, beautiful legs. Straight to pumping his aching cock inside her tight, wet channel until she screamed and begged for release. Straight to breeding. His body craved her nearly every moment of every planet rotation. But more than the loss of the sex, he missed the sound of her voice, her scent, her lovely face. He missed holding her, the sound of her soft sighs as she slept.

They hadn't had enough time together. He had barely begun to understand her. Had only seen her smile and laugh a few precious times. Had barely learned who she was—what she liked and didn't like, what her past held. Why hadn't he tried to discover these things? He'd been impatient and unkind. He'd thought her beneath him, not worthy of his time. Yet she'd still cared for him. Cared enough to anger him, to goad his worst punishment because she feared for his death.

Perhaps if they'd had more time together before the assassination attempt, he'd understand her better. He'd learn to discern her lies from truth, or to understand why she lied or who she protected. Was it her mother?

He'd demanded an update on the search for her mother daily. Daneth said the Ocretions were pretending they couldn't locate her, most likely to get more money out of him. "Then pay it," he'd shouted the last time he asked for an update. He hoped for a clue about Lamira from her mother. But even if she did not provide him with the information he sought, he wanted Lamira to have someone she loved with her. She deserved that. He'd taken her away from her mother and now imprisoned her in his guest room with very little interaction with any other beings. She must be terribly lonely. He'd refused to watch her hologram, but he felt certain she wept there in that room, all alone.

It wasn't a permanent solution. He knew he needed to make a decision about her. The decision should be to send her away. He could find a decent place for her—maybe even some underground location where humans lived free. Once he reunited her with her mother, he would send them both away.

But why did that decision make his heart ache as if it would cease to beat?

~.~

Lamira thought she would die. She'd been cooped up alone in the beautiful room for eight planet rotations, with no word or sight of Zander. Barr himself had come up a few times to serve her food—at least he missed her. He watched her eat with sad, concerned eyes. He didn't know what happened, or if he did, he didn't speak of it, but he kept an upbeat outlook, saying things like, "When the prince lets you out..."

The two servants who had helped her with the garden stopped in, bringing her small plants and showing her holograms of the rest of them.

And since she already felt dead, she considered, at least twenty times every planet rotation, telling Zander she was ready to confess the truth. She'd rather be reported to the Ocretions and executed than have him believe her unworthy of his trust. But her mother...they shared genes. If it was revealed Lamira had aberrant genes, her mother would be executed as well. She had an obligation to keep the secret her mother had worked so hard to help her hide. It wasn't just about her life.

But Zander's promise to protect her kept ringing in her ears, too. How tied to the Ocretions was he? He lived here, but his pod consisted almost entirely of Zandians. She had literally not seen an Ocretion since she arrived. Maybe he could protect her if he knew her secret. He owned her, after all. He'd bought and paid for her, fair and square. But could they take her away from him if they knew? In her experience, they could do anything they wanted. And Zander needed asylum here until he won back his own planet. No, it was best to keep her silence, even if it did mean banishment from Zander.

But she couldn't go on forever, locked in this room. She needed to beg him to let her out, to serve him still as his gardener, at least. He wouldn't have to see her. He could give her a schedule and she would be sure to never cross paths with him... although the thought made her eyes burn with tears.

She couldn't go on this way. She needed to make peace with Zander. Somehow.

Chapter Ten

Leora blinked as she returned to consciousness. A doctor with purple-hued skin and horns leaned over her, taking her blood. Her body and hair had been cleaned of the agrifarm dirt and she wore a white tunic or gown of some kind.

She licked her dry lips. "Where's...my daughter?"

She'd seen this same doctor take Lamira away from the agrifarm. It had terrified her. She'd been lucky getting placed in the agrifarm when she was pregnant with Lamira. When Johan, Lamira's father, had died in the rebellion, she'd managed to remain undetected, her position as a factory worker never questioned. The factory had closed shortly after and she'd been transferred to the agrifarm, where she kept her head down to keep them both safe. The farming required limited interaction with the guard and foremen. They didn't have to serve anyone, or scrape and grovel, or—worst of all—serve Ocretions sexually. She'd managed to hide Lamira's beauty and her claircognizance for twenty-two solar cycles there, which had been a miracle in itself.

But then, one day, Lamira had been summoned to the director's office and this doctor took her away.

The doctor didn't answer her. In fact, he pretended she wasn't speaking. Her wrists and ankles were bound to the table, so she couldn't move.

"Where's Lamira? What have you done with her?"

Her daughter was nearby. A mother knew. She'd always had a tinge of the intuition Lamira had to hide. Hunches, nudgings. She was certain, now, Lamira was here.

"Please tell me what's going on."

This, finally got the doctor's attention. He met her gaze. "You have been purchased by Prince Zander. I am sure he will tell what your duties are to be."

A tap sounded on the door, and it slid open. In the doorway stood a massive warrior of the same species. He wore a sword on his belt— a simple weapon for an advanced species. He walked in, his gait more graceful than she expected from a male of his bulk. His eyes swept over her and their gazes locked.

She caught her breath. His irises were blue, rimmed with purple—incredibly beautiful. As she stared into their depths, they darkened to a blue-violet. His horns somehow struck her as masculine and sexy, although she'd never had an affinity for any species besides her own.

The warrior cleared his throat. "Are you finished with her exam?"

"Yes."

"The prince wishes to question her."

"Tell him her health is in order—nothing good nutrition won't fix." The doctor picked up a bag and fit a tube into it. He shoved the other end into her mouth.

She jerked her head away and something sweet smelling dribbled onto her neck.

"Release her," the warrior snapped. "How can she drink when she's bound to a table on her back?"

The doctor's lips twitched, as if amused by the warrior's irritation, but the rings holding her ankle and her wrist cuffs snapped open.

The warrior walked to her side and held out a hand.

She ignored his hand and scrambled up to sit.

The warrior remained still, watching her. When she met his gaze, he inclined his head slightly in the ghost of a bow. "I am Seke." He waited and, for a moment, she wondered if he thought she ought to know him, but then she realized he was waiting for her to introduce herself.

"Leora."

He took the bag from the doctor and held it out to her. "It's not poisoned. You should drink before you meet the prince. You look thirsty."

She rubbed her cracked lips together. They were absolutely parched. She accepted the bag and drank, closing her eyes at the shock of the delicious taste. She meant to take only a sip or two, in case it was tainted, but her body overrode her mind, and she sucked on the tube, drinking deeply until half the bag had disappeared.

The warrior glowered at the doctor. "You kept her malnourished."

Once more, the doctor's lips twitched. "She cannot eat or drink when unconscious."

"Do you require food?" The warrior turned back to her, his eyebrows knit.

"No...not yet. Thank you."

Something about the warrior had disarmed her. He reminded her of Johan—pure masculinity and quiet strength. And her gut told her he could be trusted.

"Come." He beckoned her off the table and grasped her shoulders.

A shock of heat raced through her body at his touch.

He rotated her slowly to face away from him then caught her wrists and pulled them behind her back. His touch was gentle, despite the obvious strength behind it.

The cuffs clicked together and he turned her back around. She stared up at him, studying his handsome features. A piece of her hair had caught on her chapped lips, and she tried to rub it off with her shoulder.

He reached out and brushed it away. She swore his skin had turned darker purple, his horns rougher. He opened his mouth, as if he was going to say something, but then shut it again. Placing a hand at her lower back, he guided her forward. "Come, Leora. Our prince awaits."

He sure as hell wasn't her prince. But she kept her mouth shut. She needed to find Lamira—needed to know she was still alive and well.

The warrior—Seke—led her through beautiful corridors and into a giant domed room. A giant crystal was embedded in a skylight, and the light that came through was natural.

On a throne, of sorts, a young male sat. Also built of hard muscle, he had the beauty of youth. She lifted her chin and dared to look him in the face. She expected to see haughtiness there, but instead found only a haunted quality to his expression.

"Leora, chosen mate and partner of the human warrior Johan Jonas," Seke said as an introduction.

She flinched to hear him speak Johan's name. How did they know? Would they tell the Ocretions? If so, it meant her certain death.

"Daneth said to tell you she's in good health." She thought she heard disapproval in the warrior's voice—as if he disapproved of her inspection. It warmed her.

The prince cocked his head, searching the warrior with a speculative gaze.

Leora lifted her eyes to glare at him and, to her surprise, he flinched.

"I see where your daughter gets her beauty."

"Where is she? What are you doing with her?"

She expected him to ignore her questions the way the doctor had, but the prince spoke. "She is here. You will see her soon."

The prince sat back and knit his fingers. "Leora...your daughter saved my life last week."

Whatever she'd expected, it hadn't been this. She stared up in surprise.

"But she refuses to tell me how she knew of the planned assassination attempt."

Goose bumps stood up on her skin as she comprehended the situation.

"There's nothing special about my daughter," she clipped, her chin lifted. "It was probably a lucky guess."

The prince's eyes narrowed. "A lucky guess," he spat bitterly. "Yes, I've heard that from her before." He folded his arms across his chest. "Tell me, Leora, what connection do you and Lamira have with the Finn?"

The blood drained from her face, and her hands went clammy. She realized, suddenly what species they must be—Zandians. Ousted from Zandia by the Finn. A homeless species, forced to take refuge on Ocretia. "We have no connection, Your...ah Highness." She shot a quick glance at Seke.

"He is addressed as *my lord* or *Prince Zander*."

"My lord." She dropped a curtsy. "Neither Lamira nor I have any connection with other beings. We kept to ourselves on the agrifarm."

"Except for your connection to the underground human resistance movement."

She caught her breath, her heart pounding. Her throat worked as she swallowed. The prince had inside knowledge about things the Ocretion government had not yet discovered. About Johan, and the resistance. Perhaps he was not aligned with them. She took a chance, and offered the truth. "They are not connected with your enemies, my lord."

His eyebrows shot up at her admission. "What sort of information is passed?"

She swayed on her feet, feeling slightly dizzy. "The things you ask could get people killed."

"I don't work for the Ocretions."

Shivers of fear ran through her body. Her gut told her he spoke the truth—that he could be trusted, but she couldn't risk it. Not until she'd seen Lamira and knew what he wanted with them. "I wish to see my daughter."

"How did your daughter know about the assassination plan?"

She stared back at him, struggling to piece the situation together. So, the Finn had attempted to kill the prince and Lamira had saved him? She wondered if he meant anything to her.

"So you, too, refuse to answer?"

"She saved your life, my lord." She spread her palms. "You said so, yourself. Surely you cannot suspect her of treason or doubt her loyalty?"

He shook his head and stood up. "I cannot trust her."

Was that anguish on his face?

A shock of knowledge rippled through her.

He loved her. This alien cared for her daughter.

Frustration crinkled his forehead. "Take her to Lamira."

Surprised to be dismissed so easily, she dropped an uneasy curtsy. "Thank you, my lord."

"Tell your daughter she has one planet rotation to confess or I will separate and sell you both to the worst—" He stopped and pressed his lips together, and she understood. He was bluffing. And it was a lie he couldn't even finish.

Yes, he loved her.

He turned and stalked out of the room, tension radiating from the set of his shoulders and neck.

The warrior stepped forward and once more placed his hand on her lower back. A shiver ran through her. For the first time in solar cycles, her sex dampened as she thought about those hands touching her in other places.

He applied gentle pressure to turn her toward the door, guiding her forward.

"He loves my daughter." She took the risk to speak her thoughts.

The warrior halted and turned toward her. After a long moment, he said, "I believe it is true." He nudged her forward, guiding her to the hall. "But he cannot keep her if she can't be trusted."

"But she saved his life? Does that count for nothing?"

Seke made a grumbling sound. "The Zandians are an honorable species. It counts for everything. But our prince's continued safety is paramount to all else, even love. If you care for your daughter's happiness, you will convince her to speak the truth."

The warrior stopped in front of a door and pressed his palm to the screen there. The door slid open and her heart skipped a beat.

"Lamira!" she cried and ran to her daughter.

~.~

Zander stalked down the corridor and replayed the interview with Leora in his mind. One thing she said struck him as odd.

There is nothing special about my daughter.

Was it a human turn of phrase? Something he did not quite understand? Or did it mean there *was*, in fact, something special about Lamira? If so, what? In what way would she be different?

Different.

His skin crawled as a realization struck him.

Human slaves had been bred by the Ocretions for certain qualities. Docility, obedience, physical strength. Those who were found to be too intelligent, too resistant, too *special* were eliminated.

Is that what Leora had meant? Did her daughter carry special traits? Perhaps that was why Daneth's program chose her as his perfect mate. Perhaps the system had picked her, not because of some human trait, but because she had some *super*human trait. Something special. And she kept it hidden because her life depended on it. Lamira's defiance had surprised him. Did she carry other aberrant traits?

For the first time in ten planet rotations, the heaviness surrounding him lifted. He changed direction and walked briskly toward Daneth's lab.

"My lord, how did you find the new slave?"

"Her name is Leora."

Daneth took the correction in a stride. "Of course, my lord."

"Daneth, it occurred to me perhaps your program selected Lamira for me because there is something special about her genes."

"Certainly," Daneth said, as if he, too, had considered the possibility. "Her father's warrior genes would be considered out of range. If her relation to him had been known, she would have been killed."

"What if there was something else? Some special sensitivity, perhaps? An ability to predict the future? Or know things she hadn't seen?"

Understanding dawned on Daneth's expression. "A psychic ability, you mean?" He stroked his chin. "Some humans once possessed such gifts, it's possible for a recessive trait to resurface." He flicked on a holograph which projected an image of genes into the space before them. "I don't know how to search for such a gene. I would think if it was known, the Ocretions would have already found it and killed her at birth." He tapped his finger to his chin. "Show brain scan."

An image of her brain floated in the space between them.

"Compare with normal human brain activity."

An area of Lamira's brain lit up with a purple hue. "Above average activity noted," the program reported in a clipped, female voice.

"What is this area of the human brain used for?"

"Unknown."

Daneth rotated the brain image in a circle. "Show brain image of a Venusian."

The Venusians were a humanoid species with extra-large eyes and many extrasensory abilities including telepathy and energetic healing.

The Venusian brain hologram popped up. Daneth spun it around and enlarged the area that had more activity than normal in Lamira's scan. The physician's lips stretched into a grin. "Look how much this area is used." He pointed at the normal human brain scan. "Here, it is not used at all, like most of their brain mass. You were right—she has extrasensory receptor activity." His voice rose in pitch with excitement. "It makes perfect sense to breed with a female with these abilities. Think of the increased power of your offspring!"

He didn't care about his offspring at that moment. All he cared about was reclaiming Lamira.

"Thank you, Daneth. This is what I needed to know."

~.~

Lamira sat on her luxurious sleeping platform, holding both her mother's hands, still weeping with joy.

"But tell me about this prince—you are his prisoner, but he grieves your loss."

She blinked her wet lashes. "He does? How do you know?"

"I sensed it in him. He loves you. Even his warrior agreed."

"Master Seke?"

Was her mother actually blushing at the mention of the master at arms? Well, Seke was an incredible specimen of masculinity, even if he was old enough to be her father.

"But, Mother, he believes he cannot trust me."

"I know—he told me the same thing. Lamira...can you trust him?"

She hesitated. Her mother's familiar and loving face made her chest nearly explode with joy.

"He knew about your father. He knew we are part of the resistance movement, yet we both still live."

Lamira gaped in surprise. He knew? She shook her head. "Did he say why he bought you?"

Her mother shook her head. Mother Earth, which Zandian male would she be given to? Did they believe she was still of breeding age?

"Do you know why he bought me?"

"Tell me."

"For breeding. Daneth—his doctor—ran a program and it chose me as his best possible mate to bear children." She waited for the shock to appear on her mother's face. All those solar cycles her mother had worked to protect her from exactly this fate.

But her mother only touched a finger to her lips thoughtfully. "Why, do you think?"

She could not think. Her emotions were running in too many directions and her brain had overheated into a melted blob of confusion.

"I cannot see him giving the mother of his children up to the Ocretion slaughter block."

"But I haven't given him children," she wailed. "And now I won't."

"What I'm saying is perhaps he can be trusted with the truth of your gifts."

"They aren't gifts," she started to protest, but then remembered the whispering from the crystals.

He needs you. Pay attention to all knowing.

Perhaps they *were* gifts. To him, anyway. Her knowing had already saved his life, after all.

"You should tell him."

"He probably won't believe me, anyway. They don't understand sarcasm, and he's convinced humans lie about everything." She caught her mother's hand. "Wait. You know telling him may risk your life, as well."

Her mother gave her a tight smile. "I know." She squeezed her hand.

~.~

Zander paced the length of his chamber. He'd sent for Lamira and now his body hungered for her, just at the thought of having her near him again.

A tap sounded at the door. The image of Lamira standing outside with a guard, wrists bound behind her back popped up as a hologram above the door.

"Enter."

The guard walked in with her, but he dismissed him with a wave. "Leave her."

Lamira's chin was held high, defiance blazed across her delicate features. He remembered that look from the day she first arrived on his pod. She marched over to him and spat in his face.

Her attack came unexpected, so he registered only surprise, rather than anger.

"My mother will not be your sex slave!"

It was so absurd, he wanted to laugh—and she was adorable angry like this. But he didn't show amusement. Instead, he scooped her up by the waist and carried her to his sleepdisk, where he sat on the edge and draped her across his lap.

He spanked her with his hand, hard and fast. "I have no intention of using your mother as a sex slave," he made clear. "She is my guest—a boon I purchased for you after I gave you that undeserved whipping."

Lamira didn't answer, probably too caught up in wriggling under his punishing slaps.

He'd forgotten how satisfying it felt to spank her. Everything about it lit his senses on fire—the feel of her soft, supple form across his knees, the sight of her perfect little ass bouncing beneath his hand, the gasps she made each time his palm made contact. He could question her about her psychic abilities later, after her spanking. And breeding.

His wrist cuff was still programmed to monitor her arousal rate, and the numbers flashed rapidly.

Twenty percent aroused. Thirty. Thirty-five. Forty.

She liked her spankings as much as he did.

The only displeasing aspect of the situation was her clothing. He lifted her to stand between his knees and yanked down her leggings and panties. "Why are you wearing clothing? What is the rule when you enter my chamber?"

Fifty percent aroused.

Realizing he couldn't remove her shirt with her wrists bound behind her back, he grasped it with two hands at the neckline and rent the fabric down the middle, tearing it from her body.

Lamira gasped and wobbled on trembling legs. Her cheeks flushed pink with emotion, and confusion played across her face.

Sixty percent aroused.

"You are only punished in the bare, Lamira. You shall never be allowed the protection of your clothing."

Seventy percent aroused.

Her nipples stood out in stiff peaks.

He pulled her back over his knee and resumed the spanking, delighting in the contact of flesh on flesh, the crack of his palm against her bare skin, the scent of her arousal. He loved the way she squirmed over his lap, her hip rubbing his throbbing cock.

Eighty-five percent aroused.

Stars, he loved this. He loved that she grew excited when he took her in hand. He loved the heady sense of power punishing her gave him. And, yes, he loved her. He loved her. No matter what her secret, they'd work it out.

Her skin turned pink under his continued onslaught. He wondered if she could orgasm from a spanking alone. Not that it was allowed.

When he heard a sniff, he suddenly realized her back was shaking with sobs. He froze.

Oh veck. Had he spanked her too hard? He didn't think he had used more force than normal. He released her wrist cuffs.

"Lamira," he croaked, spinning her up to cradle in his arms, the way she liked it.

Her face dripped with tears, eyes red. She tucked her head against his neck, where he couldn't see her eyes.

"What happened? What's wrong?"

She shook her head, still pressed against his neck, and wept in ragged, heart-wrenching sobs. Her arousal rate had dropped back down to thirty percent.

He stroked her back and held her tight, rocking slightly. "Does it hurt too much? Should I call Daneth?"

"No," she croaked immediately.

"What do you need?"

"You!"

He stilled once more, drawing in a shocked breath. His heart beat erratically.

This was the wildness she inspired in him. A starstorm of emotions, needs, and desires.

"I've missed you, too, little human." He buried his face in her hair, rubbing his horns through the silky strands, breathing her in. She smelled both sweet and sensual, the fresh lime-citrus of her soap blending with her natural feminine musk.

He loved her.

He stood and walked on his knees up the sleeping platform, settling with his back against the wall, and his little human cradled in his lap. "I can't live without you—I don't want to. I need you here, in my chamber, between my sheets."

"I'll tell you," she sobbed. "I'll tell you everything. I promise. You may not believe me, but I'll tell you what you want to know."

He caressed her nape, pried her head from his shoulder to see her wet face. Using both thumbs, he mopped her tears. "Tell me," he murmured. "I'll believe you."

She hiccupped, trying to regain her breath. Her hand came up to cover her face from his view, but he caught her wrist. "Don't hide from me. No more lies, little slave. I want all of you—your honest truth. You're mine. Even your tears are mine."

She drew in a long, terraced breath and dashed her tears with the back of her hand. "Thank you"—she sniffed and gave a laughing sob at her own tears—"for my mother. Thank you so much."

He pulled her in and kissed her forehead. "You're welcome."

She leaned her forehead against his, looping one hand behind his neck and stroking her delicate fingers lightly over the skin there.

His body prickled with heat.

"Sometimes..." She drew in another shuddering breath. "Sometimes, I know things. About people. Not usually about the future."

"You're psychic."

Her eyes locked on his, startled. "Yes. Claircognizant. I know things I shouldn't. But since I've come here, it's been more—now I see things and hear things, too. I think it's your crystals—they've amplified the trait. You believe me?"

He traced her eyebrow, caressed her temple with the pad of his thumb. "I believe you. Your mother said something earlier today that led me to have Daneth examine your brain activity. He compared it to the Venusian brain and there were similarities."

"Do you think I have Venusian blood?"

"Daneth could probably test it to find out."

"So..." She held his favorite expression—the pleading one, with her green eyes wide. "Am I forgiven?"

He adjusted her, pulling one of her legs around so she straddled him. Her hot core pressed against his cock through his trousers, dampening them. Palming her luscious ass, he squeezed it and rocked her into him.

"I'm sorry—" His voice sounded rough—whether it was from lust or regret, he wasn't sure. "For so many things. For the times I hurt you. For—"

"No." She touched his face, stopping him. "You're a prince—the leader of your species. You were right to be cautious. Zander..."

She nibbled her bottom lip, making him want to claim her mouth, to suck that lip between his, to taste her.

"I've seen something...about us." Her gaze was intent, as if measuring whether she could tell him or not.

"Tell me. From now on, you will tell me everything. No more secrets. No, wait. I understand why you were afraid to tell me, but I will never turn you in to the Ocretions. I will not let anyone touch you—ever. You belong to me, and I protect what's mine. Understand?"

~.~

Warmth coiled in her chest, swirled up her neck. She tugged Zander's lips down to hers, attacking him, showing him how much his words affected her. He kissed her back, grasping her head and holding her still as he took over. His tongue licked between her lips, and he claimed what belonged to him.

He pushed her down to her back, crawling over her. "Tell me." His voice sounded gruff, but his eyes shone with affection. He pinned her wrists beside her head. "Now, little slave."

"I saw our baby."

His face went slack, eyes full of wonder.

Her vision blurred.

"When? I mean—"

She laughed. "I don't know. But he was perfect."

"*He?*" Zander's lips stretched into the widest smile she'd ever seen him wear. His teeth gleamed straight and white against his purple-hued skin.

She nodded. Her chest felt so full, she thought it would explode.

He nudged her knees apart and shoved down his pants, freeing his cock. "Then I guess we'd better keep breeding, so we can meet him soon."

She reached for his cock and guided him to her dripping entrance. He filled her, stretching her wide and making her gasp. After ten planet rotations without sex, she felt virginally small for his large size, despite the ample lubricant.

"Take me," he commanded, his eyes glittering with amusement. He knew, from the cuff on his arm, what his bossy commands did to her.

She arched and offered herself up to him, his for the taking. She craved his touch in every way—not only the tender caresses he'd just offered, but also this—the rough way he handled her, demanding so much yet never going too far.

He pistoned in and out of her, shoving deep on each instroke. "I missed you, naughty slave."

"I'm a good slave," she protested, giving herself over to the force of his instrokes, which rocked her up at least six inches every time.

"You spat in my face."

Oh yeah. She'd forgotten that part.

"I think, when I'm finished filling you with my seed, I will take your ass. You deserve a long, hard ass-*vecking*, don't you?"

Her head wobbled, somewhere between a nod and a shake. While she found anal sex terrifying, it had also been incredibly satisfying—the intensity equaling the pleasure.

Zander pulled out. "On your knees, hands behind your back." He shoved her torso down into the sleepdisk and lifted her hips high. She heard the click of her wrist cuffs fastening behind her legs.

She loved this position. There was something so...objectifying about it. It lifted and presented her sex and anus to him and left her face completely out of his sight.

He gripped her hips and slid into her again, resuming the hard pounding he'd been giving her. His breath grew ragged.

Her pussy gripped his cock in ecstasy.

"Come, slave."

He shoved in deep and stayed, filling her with hot streams of his cum while her pussy spasmed around his length, squeezing and milking his cock for its seed.

Despite his threat to take her ass afterward, he collapsed on top of her, releasing her wrists and laying her out on her belly. His strong arms wrapped around her from behind and he rolled them to their sides. He brushed kisses across the skin at her neck.

"I'm going to have this removed." He rubbed his thumb over the barcode tattooed at the base of her neck. "I want to make my own mark on you, Lamira."

She rolled in his arms to face him. "How?"

He leaned up on one elbow. "Would you wear my crystals?"

The fact he asked her, rather than dictated, meant something—thought she wasn't sure what. "Does that mean you would pierce me?"

He nodded, tweaking one of her nipples. "Yes. I'd pierce these. And your navel. Your ears, too, if you like." He brushed her cheek with the backs of his fingers. "You say the crystals make your intuition stronger. Perhaps wearing them will make it even more so. You'll be my own personal oracle."

"Do I have a choice?"

He stilled and his expression grew sober. "Do you not wish to be my female?"

She blinked rapidly, moisture gathering at her lashes, her chest so full it hurt. "Is that what wearing your crystals would mean?"

He nodded. "Zandian males adorn their females to show their attachment."

"I do—" Her voice cracked. "I do want to be your female, Zander."

His lips stretched into a satisfied smile. He stroked a hand up her throat to cup her chin. "I will take good care of you, little human. I promise."

Her heart thudded. She almost didn't ask it—she didn't want to ruin the moment, but she had to know. "Am I still your slave?"

He smirked. "Yes. Always, Lamira. You serve. I rule. You like it that way."

She wanted to deny it, but he had her numbers—literally—in the constant readout of his armband. "Will I ever be allowed off this pod?"

Once more, his lips curved into a wicked grin. "Only if you're a good little slave."

As always, when he reinforced his ownership over her, her pussy clenched. He tilted his head and claimed her mouth, and she lifted her lips to meet his.

Yes, she belonged to him—body and heart and soul. It wasn't perfect, but it was a start.

Epilogue

Lamira sat up, the luxurious sheets falling away from her naked form. She slept so much more now that she was pregnant, and Zander didn't mind if she spent half the morning dozing in his sleepdisk.

He sat working on his invasion plans, a hologram of his planet up and slowly rotating.

"My lord—" She could scarcely make her lips and tongue move, she'd been awakened from such a deep slumber by her knowing.

He swiveled and smiled, his eyes dropping to her swollen breasts, now pierced and adorned with his crystals.

"The being you seek is here in the pod."

He lifted a quizzical brow. "I don't understand."

Zander hadn't shared his takeover plans, but she'd gleaned enough through clairvoyance and observation.

"Do you seek someone with an army? Someone you can pay to wage a war?"

He nodded, his gaze growing sharp.

"That being is here, now. In the crystal bath." It was the one planet rotation of the week when the Zandian public were invited to use the crystal baths or visit with the prince. Zander had pushed his visitation time back to afternoon that day because the traffic had been light and he liked to spend more time with her now that she carried his child.

Zander's lip curled doubtfully. "A Zandian? With an army?"

She nodded and scooted out of bed, a sense of urgency driving her forward. "He's been here before but you have not met. I...I don't think he likes the idea of royalty. But he requires the crystal recharge all the same." She yanked on her clothing.

Zander stood and walked briskly to the door. "Will you know him when you see him?"

She swept past him into the corridor. "I'm not sure. Maybe you will." She shoved back the moment of doubt she always had about her claircognizance. There was no mistake. The feeling had been so strong.

Zander strode beside her, one hand at her lower back, the other on the handle of his sword. They reached the crystal baths just as the door slid open and a huge warrior walked out. He did not appear much older than Zander—perhaps five or ten solar cycles, but he bore scars and the lines of a being who had led a tough life.

His eyes flew open when he saw her, then took on a menacing glare. "You," he snarled.

Her heart jumped in her throat. He thought he knew her? How?

Zander shoved her behind him and slid his sword partway out of the scabbard.

The warrior ignored him, even though he was his prince and ruler. "What are you doing here, Lily? I can't imagine you think I'd ever be happy to see you again."

"You're speaking to Lamira," Zander growled.

She craned her neck around to see past her muscled master. "How do you know my sister?"

Bonus "Deleted Scene" from His Human Slave

Click here to read Lamira's piercing/mating scene with Zander. You'll also be signed up for Renee Rose's newsletter and receive free copies of **The Mayor's Discipline, Theirs to Punish, The Alpha's Punishment** and **Her Billionaire Boss** (written under her other pen name Darling Adams). In addition to the free books, you will get special pricing, exclusive previews and news of new releases.

From the Author

Thank you for reading *His Human Slave*! If you enjoyed it, I would really appreciate it if you would leave a review. Your reviews are invaluable to indie authors in marketing books so we can keep book prices down.

Other D/s Titles by Renee Rose

Regency
The Darlington Incident, *Humbled*, *The Reddington Scandal*, *The Westerfield Affair*, *Pleasing the Colonel*

Mafia Romance
The Don's Daughter, *Mob Mistress*, *The Bossman*

Contemporary
Owned by the Marine, *Theirs to Punish*, *Punishing Portia*, *The Professor's Girl*, *Safe in his Arms*, *Saved*, *The Elusive "O" (FREE)*

Western
His Little Lapis, *The Devil of Whiskey Row*, *The Outlaw's Bride*

Medieval
Mercenary, *Medieval Discipline*, *Lords and Ladies: Two Medieval Spanking Novellas*, *The Knight's Prisoner*, *Betrothed*, *Held for Ransom*, *The Knight's Seduction*, *The Conquered Brides (5 book box set)*

Paranormal
The Alpha's Promise, *His Captive Mortal*, *The Alpha's Punishment*, *The Alpha's Hunger*, *Deathless Love*, *Deathless Discipline*, *The Winter Storm: An Ever After Chronicle*

Renaissance
Renaissance Discipline

Ageplay
Stepbrother's Rules, *Her Hollywood Daddy*, *His Little Lapis*

BDSM under the name Darling Adams
Medical Play
Yes, Doctor

Master/Slave
Punishing Portia, His Human Slave

About the Author

USA TODAY BESTSELLING AUTHOR RENEE ROSE is a naughty wordsmith who writes BDSM and spanking romance novels. Named Eroticon USA's Next Top Erotic Author in 2013, she has also won *The Romance Reviews* Best Historical Romance, and *Spanking Romance Reviews'* Best Historical, Best Erotic, Best Ageplay and favorite author. She's hit #1 on Amazon in the Erotic Paranormal, Western and Sci-fi categories and is a contributor to [Write Sex Right](#) and [Romance Beat.](#) She also pens BDSM stories under the name Darling Adams

Renee loves to connect with readers! Please visit her on:
[Blog](#) | [Twitter](#) | [Facebook](#) | [Goodreads](#) | [Pinterest](#) | [Instagram](#)

Acknowledgements

Thank you for great beta reads from Aubrey Cara, Katherine Deane and Lee Savino. I appreciate Kate Richards, who pointed out just how much I like the word "just" (too much!) among other things. Thanks to Alta Hensley for dreaming up the idea of a dark non-con box set and asking me to be a part of it. Sue Lyndon designed the cover and formatted and published Human Surrender--she is and always will be my hero.

And of course, thank you, readers for indulging my master/slave fantasy!

Printed in Great Britain
by Amazon